James B. Goode

The Modern Banker

A Story of his Rapid Rise and Dangerous Designs

James B. Goode

The Modern Banker
A Story of his Rapid Rise and Dangerous Designs

ISBN/EAN: 9783744708296

Printed in Europe, USA, Canada, Australia, Japan

Cover: Foto ©Andreas Hilbeck / pixelio.de

More available books at **www.hansebooks.com**

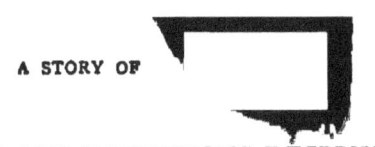

A STORY OF

HIS RAPID RISE AND DANGEROUS DESIGNS

By JAMES B. GOODE

Author of "The Belle of Wyandotte," "The Story of a Life,"
"The Union of Love," "A Trip Through Arkansaw,"
"A Farmer's Daughter," "May Blossom,"
"His Heart's Best Love," "Madge,"
"Ola," Etc., Etc.

CAGO
RR & COMPANY
TH AVENUE
1896

CHAPTER I.

"YES, wife, our boys want to marry the Caldwell girls, and have asked my permission to do
so. I do not like the idea of brothers marrying
sisters; but I know of no reason why they
should not do so,if they love each other. Neighbor Caldwell is one of our oldest and best friends,
and his family are unequaled in their education,
manners and social standing in the community.
The girls are beautiful, well-raised and healthy.
I cannot see any reason why we should object.
What do you think of it?"

"I have loved those girls all of their lives,
and unless there is some law, or some rule in
the Bible, which forbids brothers marrying to
sisters, I cannot see any reason why we should
object."

"There is no law or rule, either human or
divine, which forbids brothers marrying to sisters. I have been very careful to obtain all the
facts in the case. In fact, I find that it has
been allowed in all ages."

"I think Mamie Caldwell is one of the sweet-
est girls alive. She seems to have every quali-
fication I could ask for in a wife for Arthur.
And they will make a loving couple, I am sure.
But I am not so sure about Henry and Cora.
They are both high-tempered and domineering.
They both have black hair and eyes and both are
very ambitious. But I hope they will do well,"
said his wife.

When Farmer Hunt, as he called himself, did
anything, it was always well done, so that, when
his boys were married to the Caldwell sisters,
the infair was one of the largest ever seen in the
county. The old farmhouse was filled with
neighbors and their children, and mirth and
merriment was given full sway. The dining-
table was extended the full length of the room,
and several times filled with the merry-makers.
After supper, the dance began with a hearty
good-will, and the good old-fashioned Missouri
quadrilles, reels and galops were danced until a
late hour. Waltzing had been frowned upon by
the old-fashioned mothers of the neighborhood,
but when it was announced that Henry wanted
to waltz with his new wife, no objections were
made and the room was cleared for the performance. Neither had ever waltzed much, although
Henry had once taken dancing lessons, while

at college; and Cora had managed to take a few lessons while at school. However, the performance was watched by the assembly with the greatest interest, and, when it was over, the parents of the children discussed it among themselves. Henry and Cora took their seats with a self-satisfied air, and then turned to Arthur and Mamie, while Henry said, with a covert sneer, for he knew that neither of them waltzed, "Come, Arthur, it is now your turn to waltz with your wife."

"Please excuse us, Brother Henry, for we cannot waltz," answered Arthur.

"What a shame," exclaimed Henry, in derision, "that you would not learn, as I tried to get you to do! And, if I remember correctly, you did waltz a few times, with those Howard girls, at school. Come now, let us see how you and your wife can waltz."

"No, I know that we cannot waltz, and I do not care to make a vulgar exhibition of our awkwardness," answered Arthur.

"Perhaps you deem our waltzing a 'public exhibition of awkwardness'," said Henry, in a cold, sneering tone, while a look of intense anger came into his steely eyes.

"No, brother, I mean nothing of the kind. I simply think that my wife and I cannot waltz

well, and that it is better that we should not attempt to do so; especially,since I know that the
general opinion of all of our friends here is
against this mode of dancing."

The signs of general approval which followed
this speech made it impossible for Henry to
control his temper,and he rose and said: "Come,
wife, we will retire to our room and let this
saintly crowd of old fogies enjoy their innocent
amusements and gossip our characters away
from us. They are my father's guests, hence
you must allow me to excuse their ignorance and
vulgar ways. They have never been anywhere,
nor have they seen anything of the world. They
do not know that waltzing is one of the greatest
accomplishments in good society, and that none
but fanatics and prudes object to it among the
upper classes. You may rest assured, my dear
Cora, that I shall not settle among such a set.
I will move to the city, where we can associate
with people who are more congenial to our tastes.
Allow us to bid you good-night." Then, before
any one could say a word, Henry took his wife
by the arm and marched upstairs to their room.
But when they reached the secrecy of their
chamber, Cora clung to his arm and burst into
tears, as she said, "Oh, Henry, I am so sorry
that you have so grievously insulted all of our

friends! I feel that they will never forgive us."

"Do not be a fool, Cora! Don't you see that they have wantonly insulted us, and that it was my duty to resent it, if I want them to respect us?"

"I am so sorry we danced that nasty waltz. I did not want to do it, but you insisted, and now all of my friends will desert me because of it all."

"I am not sorry in the least. I am really glad it has all happened as it has. I had made up my mind to cut the whole lot of them and move away; and this will give us a good excuse for doing so, at once. We will start on our wedding tour to-morrow morning and I will begin seeking a position in the city."

The young wife was too much pained to argue the matter, so they went to bed in silence. Her heart was aching and her tears were falling silently, as she placed her head on her pillow; where, long after the surly husband had gone to sleep,she lay and grieved over the destruction of her friendship for all of those downstairs, whose love she had enjoyed from childhood. Poor woman! Her idol had been rudely shattered, before she had been married two days. And as the hours of night slowly passed away, all of the best part of her life became as a dream. She

knew that, from henceforth, she would be a
changed being.   It seemed to her that such a
gratuitous insult could only emanate from one
who was naturally cold-hearted, and she felt
that she never could enjoy a real affection for
her husband.   Her womanly intuition opened
up the doors of a cold life for her, and she wept
the night away, contemplating its horrors.

When Henry and his wife left the room, Arthur
arose and expressed his sorrow at the untoward
event which had transpired, and tried to excuse
his brother's insulting language to his friends,
as best he could.   But all felt that it would be
best to go home, and the house was soon deserted, except by its inmates.   Henry's mother
was heartbroken.   His father, who was an old-
fashioned Christian, swore that Henry was no
longer a son of his, and the neighbors were almost universal in their feelings of resentment
against him.

When Arthur and Mamie reached their room,
she threw her arms around his neck and kissed
him tenderly, as she said: "Arthur, dear, you
cannot think how much I was relieved when
you so nobly refused to make me try to waltz.
It would have been in such bad taste to have
done so, in the presence of all four of our par-

they were so much opposed to waltzing. It would have been such a poor return for your father's kindness, for you know that he was hard to persuade to let us dance at all. But I am sorry that Henry became so much offended."

"Yes, my love, it is all very sad; but let us not talk of it. I am too happy to allow Henry's hot temper to make me unhappy long. You know I am used to his ways and do not worry over them."

"Oh, I am so glad that you are not like him! I know that I would break my heart, if you were. But I do not think Cora will care so very much. I am almost sure they will fight before long; for Cora has had her own way all of her life, and she has the most violent temper I ever heard of. But at heart she is as good as gold. She will have her own way, but if you will allow her to do so without opposition, no one can be more loving or kinder than she is."

"Let us hope they will get along all right," he answered, and then they went to sleep, as happy as ever any couple were, under similar circumstances.

Henry and his wife took their wedding tour, without being very happy over it. He succeeded in getting a position as clerk in a new banking house which was just starting up in the city,

and he and his wif[...]ed rooms and
board in one of th[...]ment boarding
houses, where one [...]acquainted with
the inmates, which [...]d in all large
cities. The nove[...]ituation rather
amused Cora at fi[...]long she found
that life in a boardi[...]ut a dreary existence at best. [...]y was not absolutely unkind to he[...]s so completely
her master in every[...]she often won-
dered what had bec[...]much vaunted
temper of former da[...]

Henry Hunt was[...]an. Cold, cal-
culating and not ov[...]with conscience,
he had determined [...]rtune, honestly,
if possible; but to [...]e at all events,
if it could be done [...]ally committing
any offense agains[...]He was a very
observant man, an[...]first day of his
clerkship in the ba[...]made the study
of the business of b[...]business of his
life. In three mon[...]had thoroughly
mastered all of the [...]of the business,
and was really the[...]man in the establishment, with t[...]of Mr. Lyman
himself, who was a[...]well versed in
all of its tricks an[...]les, as well as
being conversant w[...]eories, designs

and calculations of all of the great money-lords
of the world. Andrew J. Lyman was an English
Jew, whose ancestors had intermarried into some
of the families of several of the great financial
masters in England. He had been reared and
educated with the sole intention of being a
banker, and had spent his life in the study of all
of the intricacies of financial lore. He was now
about thirty years of age, and had come out to
America to establish a small bank, which, it was
his intention, should become the corresponding
bank of all of the banks under the influence of
his great relatives back in England, all of whom
had the most implicit confidence in his honesty
and ability to manage their interests in this
country. In this way he expected to control
vast sums of money, which he would be able to
handle to his own advantage, as a banker. However, his own capital was limited to about $10,-
000, and he felt the need of increasing it·by taking in a partner. It was necessary that he should
place his little bank on an unequivocal basis, before he could afford to ask his relatives for their
business. Yet he was a very cautious man,
given to be suspicious of all men and things,
unless he was secured against the possibility of
loss. It was necessary that he should take in a
partner, but he wanted one peculiarly fitted for

his business. His partner must be a partner only in results. He must be a servant in the business, whose duty it must be to do the will of his superior, without asking too many questions. But it was necessary that this partner should be really posted as to the business of banking, and such men were hard to find.

Mr. Lyman had opened his banking house under the firm name of Andrew J. Lyman & Co., as a private savings bank, with $10,000 capital, which of course was all furnished by him. When Henry Hunt applied to him for employment, he made inquiries and found that he was the son of a wealthy farmer in the interior, and that he had married the daughter of another wealthy farmer in the same locality. These were points in his favor, and when, after carefully questioning him, he found that he was intelligent, active, versatile and ambitious, he decided to employ him. Closer acquaintance proved to him the wisdom of his choice. He at once began educating Henry in the rules of the banking business, and found him an apt scholar; so, at the end of three months, he had decided that Henry Hunt was the man he wanted for a partner, if he could only raise enough money.

One morning, Henry was called into Mr. Lyman's private office, when the following conversation was had between them:

"Henry, what do you consider the best property that a man can invest his means in?"

"I can hardly say, sir, but I would like to hear your ideas on that point."

"Well, you know that cash money is the only kind of property that all men desire. Every living man is your customer when you deal alone in actual cash. Everybody wants it. They all must have it. They will give you any other property they may have for it, and give you a margin of profit, for the exchange. Thus you see that the man who invests his means in actual cash money has the best property in the world. It will obtain all things. It is easily carried from place to place. It has no strings tied to it. It passes at par all over the world. Cash money is subject to no discounts. It has no diseases. It never dies."

"But, sir, if a man places his means in cash money, and does not invest it, it will make him nothing."

"Correct. But when a man has actual cash at all times, it gives him a great advantage over the man who has any other property; because the demand for the cash is much greater than for any one thing else. Everybody must have cash, at times, so the dealer in cash can always speculate. The demand never ceases, it is unlimited. This demand enables the dealer in cash to name his own terms and security. If he is shrewd, he takes every advantage and precaution. A man is a fool, if he loses anything when he is dealing in cash money. Then the man who can control the greatest amount of cash, is the surest to make a fortune. The banking business not only allows a man to loan out his own money; but the security of his vaults induces his neighbors to leave their cash with him, free of charge; and he can loan out a large per cent of their money and get interest on it, which he can apply to his own account."

After a long conversation, on the lines laid down above, Mr. Lyman made Henry Hunt the offer to take him into the bank, make him cashier at a liberal salary, and put him in a sure way to make a fortune, if he could raise $10,000 cash to pay for a one-half interest in the bank.

"But that will be impossible, sir, for I have no money, and no possible way to make any, or get it."

"You have wealthy relatives. Will they not aid you?"

"I fear not, sir," Henry answered, as he thought of the gratuitous insult that he had heaped upon them before he left home. "I understand that they have helped my brother to buy a fine farm; but—"

"Then you are entitled to as much as your brother. Go down there and demand your rights. Send your wife down on a month's visit and let her prepare them for your arrival. Dress her out in silk. Give her some diamonds and fine jewelry. I will let you have the money if you need it. Go down and impress them with your own importance. Prove to them that this is the chance of your lifetime. When they see these signs of prosperity, they will let you have the money."

After following his instructions to the letter, Henry sent his wife down to the old homestead in grand style. She was thoroughly posted on the matter at hand, and entered into all the plans with a will.

Henry had but little faith in the expedition, but he was very anxious to get the money. He was determined to do all in his power to succeed, and his wife's letters gave him some hope of success, when he started a month after she had gone down there.

CHAPTER II.

CORA HUNT was kindly received by her old friends, and enjoyed her visit to her parents very much. That she was sadly changed, they all saw at a glance. Instead of being the careless, happy girl they had known, she was now a woman of fashion, a formal creature, with whom very few of her old friends could get in sympathy. That her husband had made a success, was evident. Reports had often reached them to that effect. But while they could not feel at ease in her presence, all of her old friends did all they could to make her enjoy her visit. She was never an especial favorite, but she had always been well received, and thus it seemed that the neighbors were ready to overlook the insult that had been placed on them the night of her infair, and receive her and her husband with the best grace possible.

When Henry Hunt arrived he met his wife at the residence of his brother Arthur, where all the evidences of happiness and prosperity, which abounded, caused him to feel envious of his brother's good fortune. However, he carefully guarded his expressions on this point.

Henry's parents received him with a studied courtesy but with no cordiality, but Cora's parents seemed to take considerable pride in their "children from the city."

After a few days spent in visiting, Henry broached the subject of the money to his father and father-in-law, while all three were together at the latter's home. He explained his prospects in glowing terms, mentioning the fact that he supposed they would be willing to aid him, at least with as much money as they had given to his brother and sister-in-law. After holding a consultation, the two fathers explained that they had only given Arthur and Mamie $2,500 each, or a total of $5,000, while he had gone in debt $5,000 more on his farm. They expressed a willingness to do as much for him, but both declined to do more, as they did not have the money and did not know where they could get it. To this he replied, that, if he could get them to sign notes for $2,500 each, he felt assured that he could get the bank to carry these amounts, until such time as it might suit them to pay them. To this they were forced to reluctantly agree, and Henry carried $5,000 in cash and $5,000 in good bankable five-year notes, back to Mr. Lyman.

"Henry will take care of those notes himself, don't you think, neighbor Hunt?" asked Mr. Caldwell, a few days later.

"I hope so, but I am free to say that I do not like the shape this matter has left me in. I had just gotten out of debt, and had laid up a little money for my children. I was perfectly willing to divide the money between them, but I am sorry I signed that note."

"So am I, since you mention it. It leaves me in bad shape, for I have no money, and I begin to feel that old galling feeling of debt stealing over me again."

"Yet I do not see how we could have done otherwise."

"Neither do I, neighbor, neither do I."

But there was a shadow of trouble on their faces as they parted.

Henry's face beamed with satisfaction, when Mr. Lyman accepted the notes and cash and issued to him $12,500 worth of the stock in the bank, which was now capitalized for $25,000, instead of for $20,000, as Henry expected would be the case.

"We can turn in the first $5,000 of our surplus to complete our payments on stock. I preferred to make the capital $25,000," explained Mr. Lyman. "And now, Henry, we had better decide on our salaries. What amount would you suggest as suitable remuneration for our services, you as cashier and myself as president?"

"I am willing for you to decide that point. I feel assured that I could get along on my old salary of $100 per month, but perhaps you might need—"

"I say $100 per month! As equal owner in this bank, it will be necessary for you to take a fine residence in the best residence portion of the city. No, sir, I know that you cannot live on less than $5,000 per annum. As for myself, I have no inclination to try to live on less than $5,000 per annum."

"But can we afford to vote ourselves a salary of $10,000 per annum, while our capital stock is only $20,000—I mean $25,000?"

"Well, let us calculate a little," answered Mr. Lyman. "Our last statement shows average deposits of $140,000, which, added to the capital stock now, shows $165,000. Our loans and discounts are now $125,000, at an average rate of ten per cent, making the gross income $12,-500. The profits on our short-time brokerage more than pays our expenses, so you see that when we vote ourselves a salary of $5,000 each, we have $2,500 per annum left to declare as a dividend—just making ten per cent dividend on

our capital stock. You see, everybody does
not stop to make this calculation. They merely
read in the papers that such and such a bank
has declared a dividend of ten per cent per
annum. The salaries of the officers go into the
expense account, and in this way the public
never knows what a bank is really making. In
our case, if we voted ourselves small salaries,
we would have to declare a dividend of about
forty per cent per annum on our capital stock.
This would never do in the world. It would
cause the people to rise and vote the banks out
of existence, if they knew what immense profits
are really made."

When Henry Hunt arrived at home that
evening, he was in a mood for reflection. He remembered that it had taken his father twenty-
five years to save up $15,000 farming, and yet
he was considered one of the most successful
farmers in the county. He also thought of all
the bankers he had ever known, and in every
case he saw those bankers rapidly rise to wealth
and position. And by making a careful com-
parison among all of his acquaintances, he saw
that the bankers were the only class of people
in America who were enjoying an era of universal prosperity. He recognized the fact that
prices had been generally declining on every

product produced by human skill and labor, while money and its equivalent, bonds, mort-gages, debts, etc., had been gradually rising. Now, he thought, there must be a cause for all this. Nothing comes by chance. He made up his mind to find out these causes. Finally he arose, saying: "Father is a fool! He ought to quit farming and go into the banking busi-ness. But then, all the farmers are fools, on the subject of finance."

CHAPTER III.

THE United States was now passing through the bloody civil war of 1861. Its baneful influence had been felt on the characters in this story, just as they were by almost every other family in the country. Arthur Hunt, who was a citizen of Missouri, took sides with the ill-fated rebels, and bravely marched at the head of his company, first, and at the head of his regiment, later, during all the time it lasted. He was a born leader of men, broad-shouldered, with a fine, open countenance, high forehead, dark curly hair, and a demeanor that would have gained respectful admiration in any army; it was no wonder that he rose rapidly. As colonel of his regiment, he was loved and honored by both officers and men. He was ever ready for the call of duty, braving all dangers and shirking nothing, as none but Nature's noblemen can do in such trying times. Farmer Hunt' and Farmer Caldwell went out in Arthur's company, and as they saw the great honors that were being heaped upon him, they felt a great pride in their boy. Col. Arthur Hunt was a modest man. He did not seem to see those honors, nor did he allow them to cause him to feel one moment of exultation. His heart beat proudly at the thought of doing his duty bravely, and he never wavered from it. But his heart was sorely troubled. While he was away on the field of battle, things were going very badly at home. His fair, sweet young wife had done all that she could to keep the farm up, and had succeeded in keeping the interest on the mortgage paid. But now the mortgage was due and its payment had been demanded of her.

More than this, came the fact that the notes given by both his father and his father-in-law, to aid his brother Henry to get into the banking business, were now due and payment had been demanded by Mr. Lyman, as agent for the English holders of the same. Of course, all of these demands were worded in the kindest and most polite terms, expressing the hope that it would not be a hardship for them to pay the amounts at that time, but reiterating the positive demand for immediate payment.

Colonel Hunt called his father and his father-in-law into his tent for a consultation, and after due consideration, they decided that their only hope was to apply to Henry, at New York, and ask him to carry the paper for them. This was done, and in due time an answer was received, stating that it was almost impossible for him to obtain money to loan on property located in any of the states now in rebellion, but after much trouble he had finally obtained the promise of the money, on the following terms: First, his father's note would be carried one year, if he would sign the enclosed mortgage on his entire farm (well worth $10,000), to secure the payment of the $2,500. He could also carry his father-in-law's $2,500 note one year, if he would sign the enclosed mortgage on his farm (which was well worth $10,000),to secure it. In regard to his brother's debt, he found that it was utterly impossible for him to obtain over $4,000 on his farm, but that if Arthur could manage to raise $1,000 and pay on his note, and would then sign the enclosed mortgage for $4,000, secured on his farm (which was worth $10,000), he could get it carried for one year.

Another consultation was held, and it was decided that Colonel Hunt had better get a leave of absence and go home and arrange the matter the best he could. However, the two old men signed the mortgages and gave them to him, to be used if he found it necessary.

This visit home was the first he had made during the two years the war had been in prog-

ress, and his heart ached when he saw the desolation which had fallen upon the entire country.
Husbands and fathers were away in the war.
Farms were uncultivated; fences, barns, houses
and other improvements had been destroyed by
the armies of both sides, and, worse still, the
state was being overrun by a set of guerrillas,
under the facetious title of "home-guards."
These inhuman fiends levied tribute from the
poor women and outraged every feeling in the
breast of the honorable soldier. His own home,
being a little off from the main road, had not been
visited yet, but those of his father and father-
in-law had been badly used. Not a horse or farm
beast remained. His mother and mother-in-law
had taken up their homes with his wife, and the
three ladies were in the last stages of despair
when he arrived.

When Colonel Hunt learned the real situation,
he organized a company of boys and old men
and made a determined attack on the guerrillas,
whom he vanquished, with but little loss. He
then organized relief parties and sent them all
over the county to relieve the prevailing distress
of the people. Through his influence, crops
were planted and the county was placed on a
self-supporting basis. When these reforms were
accomplished he turned his attention to his

own affairs, and finally succeeded in obtaining
a loan of $1,000, which enabled him to forward
all of the mortgages to his brother in New York,
who accepted them and forwarded the old notes
and mortgage to him, with a strict injunction to
be sure to be ready to take them all up when
they fell due, a year hence; as he felt assured
that it would be impossible for him to get any
more extensions. Henry complained bitterly
of the hard times, said it was almost impossible
for him to get this money this time, and gave
them all full notice that he would not undertake
the matter again at all. He explained that if he
had the money, himself, he would take pleasure
in carrying the paper for all three of them, until the war was over, etc., etc. It was a char-
acteristic letter and showed plainly that unless
these notes were paid when due, Henry would
desert them all and the three farms would have
to be sold. Thus it was, that Colonel Hunt
returned to his regiment with a heavy heart.
But he carried the blessings and respect of all
of his old neighbors and friends with him. Yet,
however grand or noble these felicitations and
honors may be, they will not pay mortgages.

It is necessary that we should now take up
the story of Henry's life, where we left off.
The reader will remember that he had just se-

cured a half interest in the bank of Andrew J. Lyman & Co., of New York, and that the partners had just voted themselves $5,000 salary each, per annum. As before stated, Henry was a shrewd man, and the reader may be assured that he did not spend over $100 per month. He had no idea of taking an expensive establishment, nor did he give himself any airs on account of his rise in the world. He drew his salary regularly, but he established a pawn-shop, down on the Bowery, where he employed one of those conscienceless chattel-mortgage fiends to extract ten per cent interest per month, off the unfortunate, who were forced to pledge three times as much value as they received, as security for the "loan." This shop turned out to be a veritable gold-mill. To illustrate the methods adopted: A gentleman offered a gold watch, which had cost him $100, and asked for a loan of $50 on it. The watch was examined carefully, and its owner was then informed that it would be impossible to make a loan for over $25 on such a watch. The man was compelled to have the money, felt assured that he could easily repay the loan inside of the thirty days allowed to redeem it in, and, of course, was forced to accept the $25. By actual reports, one-third of all such customers as this never return before the time expires, and the watch is sold for about $75 cash. The other two-thirds of such customers come in at the end of thirty days, pay $2.50 interest, one dollar for papers and 50 cents for insurance, none of which cost the pawnbroker anything, making a total of $29 he pays for his watch. This gives the pawnbroker $4 interest on $25 for 30 days' time, giving him 192 per cent interest per annum. Thus we see the reasons why Henry Hunt was rising so rapidly in the world. Now, we do not mean to say that all bankers are doing this way, but many of them are.

Mr. Lyman was well pleased with his partner. He had found him an active, shrewd, careful man, of unusual ability as a banker. At the end of one year's time, he decided that it would be best to increase the capital stock of the bank to $50,000, and his satisfaction knew no bounds when he found that Henry came up with his $12,500 cash without any trouble. Like Henry, Mr. Lyman had been running a pawnshop—on Union Square. So he, too, was ready with his $12,500, and the bank capital stood at $50,000.

Once more we see the partners in consultation:

"I think we had better increase our salaries a little, hadn't we, Henry?" said Mr. Lyman.

"I suppose it would be better, for the dividends will be very high unless we do," he answered.

"What are our average deposits?"

"About $350,000."

"And our loans and discounts are—?"

"About $250,000, at ten per cent per annum."

"And the profits on our short-time brokerage?"

"Will more than pay all expenses."

"Then we will vote ourselves $10,000 per an-
num each, as a salary. This will leave us $5,-
000 to declare as a dividend of ten per cent per
annum on our stock."

To this Henry readily agreed, and the confidential clerk was informed that his own salary
would be raised to $150 per month, and the
meeting of the stockholders was over. Mr.
Lyman now applied to his wealthy kinsmen in
England for their business, and in due time was
apprised that they had placed his bank on their
books as their correspondent at New York City,
and would send a deposit of $100,000, to place
to their credit.

CHAPTER IV.

THE war had now been going on about a year. The president of the United states had called for recruits several times, and then had made a general levy on all of the Union States for troops. Mr. Lyman and Henry came to the front, as soon as this levy was made, and patriotically—sent substitutes.

A few days after this, Mr. Lyman called Henry into their private office and said: "Henry, my boy, my relatives in England propose to do great things for us. But, as in all vast matters of finance, we must use the greatest . discretion and secrecy. The bankers of Europe are watching the progress of this war with great interest. President Lincoln has applied to them for a large loan, and they are not ready to advance the money to this government until they receive certain concessions from Congress. You and I have discussed the poor basis we have for real banking in this country. There is a tendency toward governmental money. This must be checked. The banks must obtain the right to make and control all of the money we use, except gold coin and subsidiary silver. If the banks can do this, they will be able to control the flow of the money to suit their own interests. In order to accomplish this, it will be necessary that Congress shall pass a law, offering bonds of the government for sale. These bonds must be made the basis of a new banking law, giving the right to make bank notes, as money, to the banks. European bankers expect American bankers to stand by them in this matter, and it is our duty to do so. I have just received the following very important circular. Read it."

Mr. Lyman then handed the famous "Hazzard Circular" to Henry Hunt, who, after glancing at the head and signature, read aloud as follows:

"Slavery is likely to be abolished by this war, and chattel slavery destroyed. This, I, and my friends, are in favor of, for slavery is but the owning of labor, and carries with it the care of the laborer; while the European plan, led on by England, is for Capital to control Labor, by controlling the Wages. *This can be done by controlling the money.* The great debt that Capitalists will see to it· is made out of the war, *must be used as a means to control the volume of money. To accomplish this, the bonds must be used as a banking basis.* We are now waiting for the Secretary of the Treasury to make this recommendation to Congress. *It will not do to let the Greenback, as it is called, circulate, as money, any great length of time, as we* CANNOT CONTROL THAT."

"What do you think of it, Henry?"

"It coincides with my views exactly. Where did you get it?"

"I received it in my confidential mail this morning, from my relatives and banker-friends in England. They intimate that they may desire to place a few millions in these bonds, and say that they will immediately ship us one million dollars in gold, to be held by us, subject to our check, and insist on our using this money to obtain the passage of such laws as their interests may demand, from time to time. You understand that this shipment was merely a donation, made by all of them, to be used for 'campaign purposes.' I will leave for Washington to-morrow morning, to begin operations. It will be necessary to establish an expensive lobby there, the details of which I propose to settle on this trip. I am satisfied that it will be useless to attempt to use any money trying to gain a point with President Lincoln. But I may gain something by approaching the Secretary of the Treasury. I shall attempt it, at all events. One thing I feel sure of; we must succeed in getting a number of Congressmen on our side. I will put my lobby-workers at work securing influence at once."

"Yes, Mr. Lyman, that is the plan. You must be devilish sly about all this, so that if it ever gets into the papers, no shadow shall ever appear against us or our friends."

"To be sure. You can trust me to do that."

"I know it, sir, I know it. I have no fear that you will ever make a false step, in any way."

"Now that I shall have my hands so full of these important matters, almost the entire management of the bank will fall on your shoulders, Henry; but, like the prophet of old, 'I know in whom I have trusted.' I have no fears of you. With more than a million dollars at your own absolute disposal all the time hereafter, I expect you to do grand things this year. We ought to be able to declare a fair dividend and still vote ourselves a salary of $50,000 each next year."

"I shall do my best, sir. You can rest assured of that."

"I know it, my boy, I know it. And, in the meantime, I ought to be able to save a few thousands for our benefit, out of the millions I expect to spend in Washington; and of course

we divide that between us.   We are partners in
everything, Henry; partners in everything."

"Certainly.   I shall   run   the business here.
You will look after our interests in Washington.
We divide profits on everything.   That is un-
derstood."   .

With a salary of $20,000 per annum, and
about as much profit from his pawn business,
Henry decided that it was his duty to take an
elegant residence and force himself and family
to the front among the leading financiers of
New York.   The fact that their bank had been
chosen by the money-lords of England, to dis-
tribute the lobby funds, had already drawn considerable comment to the owners of this bank;
so Henry found that he was gladly received,
when he demanded admittance into the charmed
circle.   His wife had thoroughly educated herself in all of the ways of fashion.   She was
naturally fastidious, eager for dress and the
pomp and vanities of the world, and she was a
great aid to Henry in carrying out his great
plans about this time.   While Cora did not
possess the sweet, womanly beauty of her sister
Mamie, she was undoubtedly one of the hand-
somest ladies in New York.   But one thing
marred her face, and, on studying it carefully,
a good observer of character would have de-

cided that her soul was asleep, that her affections
had been crushed, that she was a little bit disgusted with the world, as she had found it. But
she had a queenly way about her that won her
many compliments. She had the lively gait of
the fast set, and was fast learning the most de-
voted ways of the extra-ultra-unutterables. Her
diamonds were not so costly as those some of
the ladies of New York wore, but she wore them
with a better grace. Her dresses did not come
from Worth's, but they seemed to become her
better than those of that celebrated milliner did
her friends. Thus it was, that when Cora Hunt
appeared in her residence on Fifth Avenue,
there were few ladies in New York who were
more eagerly sought after than she was. With
his usual good judgment, Henry had secured a
lease on a most desirable house, well located,
on very reasonable terms; so the reader need
feel no uneasiness about his not being able to
keep up the style that he had adopted. With
the utmost skill, he managed to keep up with
the families of millionaires, at a cost that would
have seemed nominal to any very wealthy man.
Every cent was made to count. Everything was
sacrificed for a brilliant show of wealth before
the world; while, really, a miser's hand was
closely guarding every expense, in private.

His wife had been so completely subdued that she had almost lost her own personality. In public, they were the most attentive couple alive. In private, Cora felt herself one of the most miserable women in the world. Their home relations were cold. Neither of them seemed to care what the other did, except in public. Henry spent most of his leisure hours at his club. Cora spent hers at the theater or at other places of amusement, with a coterie of friends with whom she was a favorite. It is true that, at times, Henry appeared at these places, and escorted her home with the greatest ceremony. But Cora was proud and ambitious, and there was no danger of her doing anything that would have compromised her position in society, in any way. Henry knew this and was content.

Cora was very much surprised, therefore, when Henry insisted on her going on a visit to her old home, during the summer of the last year of the war. He gave her no reason for this request, except that he was anxious to hear all of the news and did not have time to make the visit himself. This being the case, he could not see any reason why she should not make the visit, see all of her old-time friends, and have a vacation from the turmoils of fashionable life, which, he assured her, he thought were beginning to weary her. At first she did not like the idea much. She felt that a great and almost impassable gulf had come between her and her old friends. She felt that it would be hard for her to accommodate herself to the smallness of the existence she would be compelled to endure down there for three weeks. But at last a thought of her old parents came to her. She remembered that she had slighted them with impunity, during the five years of her life in New York. She remembered that it had been over a year since she had heard a word from them. She had never been a good correspondent, and since their letters had been filled with news of the war and of their troubles, she had failed to answer the letters and they had ceased. With the conscious superiority of self-made people, she felt herself immeasurably above the relatives and friends of her childhood days. She had no patience with them. They ought to have made a fortune and a position in the world, as her husband had done, if they wanted to retain her friendship. They had not done this, and were therefore unworthy of attention from her. But she obeyed her husband and made the visit. Let future chapters explain the results.

CHAPTER V.

CORA HUNT had no idea of the trials and troubles which had beset her relatives in Missouri. She expected to see the old place look about the same as usual. She thought the house would look a little older, and expected to find the family looking somewhat older. She had an idea that she would hear the chickens cackling and the cows lowing, as of old.

Her sister Mamie met her at the depot, and the two drove back alone in a single one-horse buggy. The road led by both of the old homesteads, and the sisters discussed the situation as they drove along. Cora asked no questions about the old places and Mamie did not mention the condition they were in until they made the turn to drive up the old avenue of elms, at her father's home, when Cora exclaimed: "Where is the house?"

"It was burned down two years ago, by the guerrillas. The Yankees had driven off all of the stock a few days before, and mother had come over to stay with me. One night we saw

40

a great fire and knew that the old house was gone. It was a wonder they left the barn."

Tears stood in their eyes as they drove about the old place and looked at all the desolation around them. They were the first tears that Cora had shed for a long time, and the emotions which filled her breast were the noblest she had felt for many months. Her sister told her all of the story of their distress, while they wandered among the ruins of their once happy home. For the first time in her life, she felt the emptiness of the existence she had passed through during the last five years.

They drove by the homestead of Farmer Hunt, and while the old house was still standing, it had been so badly defaced that it looked, if possible, more desolate than the home of their parents. Weeds had grown up around the yard, doors and window-shutters were gone and the out-houses had all been pulled down for wood to burn while the passing armies had been camped there. There was a small field of corn growing on each one of the old farms, which the members of the relief committees had planted and worked, which was the only sign of life on either place. It was a sad sight, and it gave Cora the horrors to observe it all.

At last they reached the residence of Colonel

Hunt, and here Cora determined to brighten up; so she said:

"Ah, Mamie, I see that you are a better farmer than our mothers are. Still, I see that your place looks like a 'widow woman's place.'"

"Yes, we have been able to make a living, with the aid of little Pompey, a little negro boy that was given to Arthur last year, by an old planter, whose farmhouse was saved from the flames by Arthur's order. And really I do not know what I should have done without the little ape. You will soon see him, and you must remember that he considers himself the head of this family, and make due obeisance to him. He is the only 'man pusson,' as he terms it, on the place. He is the greatest worker I ever saw, and has worked sixty acres of corn this year, with what little aid mother and myself could give him. Mother Hunt is in very delicate health, and could not work in the field at all."

"Do you mean to say that you have actually worked in the field, yourself, and allowed our mothers to do so?"

"Why, certainly. Look at my hands."

"Why did you not apply to me? Didn't you know that I would have aided you?"

"I preferred to work, rather than beg."

"What became of your husband's pay for soldiering?"

"I had to use that to pay the interest on the three mortgages, and to pay back the $1,000 which Arthur borrowed, in order to pay the old mortgage down to $4,000, so that Henry would take it up and extend it."

"Does Henry own those mortgages now?"

"Yes, his bank does. I sent him the last interest last month, and really I thought for awhile that he was going to sell all of the farms, for he at first refused to extend the notes another year. But at last, when all of the neighbors joined in a petition to him, he agreed to extend them one year longer, if I would pay up the interest in advance. I was compelled to do this, and had to use the money that I had intended to buy our winter's clothes with, in order to do it. But I suppose that we can get along some way."

At this point, they drove up to the front gate, just as Pompey sprang forward to hold the horse, saying:

"Be so obnoxyus as to git out, ladies. I'se sorry my master ain't arriv yit, er he would er be glad to er extol to yer er more illiberate welcome."

"But I am here to welcome my own sister, Pompey. Let me introduce you to my sister, Mrs. Cora Hunt, Pompey."

"Shore, now, Miss Mamie, you don't 'spect

me to belebe dat dis here lady am yer own sister. Youse foolin' me."

"Why, certainly she is my sister. Why not?"

"Because she don't look er little bit like yer. You see, Miss Cora is all decked out like my young missus, down Souf, only she didn't paint and powder like dat."

Both ladies laughed at Pompey's gibes, and then made their way into the house, where Cora was welcomed heartily by her mother-in-law, but with some constraint by her own mother, whose heart rebelled at the sight of so much "finery," as she termed it, while she was in such dire distress. She made a mental compari· son of her daughters, and was forced to the con· clusion that the loving, free-hearted, anxious-to-aid-her-parents Mamie, even in her distress and poverty, was much more beautiful and noble than her painted sister of fashion. She remembered that it was signing a note to aid Henry to get into the bank that had caused all of her distress. She felt that it was the duty of her daughter to try to alleviate her position, but was too proud to say so. Henry's mother, on the other hand, laid all the blame on her boy, and made up her mind to be kind to his wife, but never to speak to Henry again. She knew that it was Henry's duty to turn over the mortgage on his father's farm at once, for she knew that the original note had only been signed as a favor to Henry, that he might be enabled to get into the bank. She had long since been forced to confess that Henry was heartless, or he would never have accepted the money that was intended to buy his own mother's winter clothes, as interest on that debt which was made as a favor to him. And when he continued to threaten to foreclose this mortgage, she felt that he could no longer be a son of hers.

CHAPTER VI.

UNDER all of these circumstances, it was no wonder that Cora felt that her reception ought to have been different. She, the petted belle of a great city, felt that she ought to have been made much of in her childhood's home. She saw at a glance that her own mother appeared nervous, that she was not cordial in her greetings and that it seemed to be impossible for her to get in sympathy with her. Mother Caldwell was hale and hearty, but she bore some marks of trouble on her noble brow. She had always been a woman of decided character. There was never any doubt about her position on any subject that was near to her heart. Mother Hunt, who was never very stout, had been much troubled over the idea of that mortgage, and her pale, delicate features bore decided marks of grief, while her eyes wore a haunted look of almost despair. The fact that her husband and one of her sons had been away from her for almost four years, exposed to all of the perils and hardships of war, had been a severe blow to her health and spirits. She also mourned

over the destruction of her beloved home and
the loss of all of her well-known farm animals.
But it was the fact that her boy—yes, deny it as
much as she might, she knew that Henry was
still her son—had deserted her in her old age
and poverty,and had taken a mean advantage of
his own father,and brought them to the brink of
ruin by his exacting demands for the payment
of a note that was made for no other purpose
than to aid him in his struggles to get a start in
life,—to think that she had nursed a being who
would treat her in this way, seemed more than
she could bear. This thought was always with
her.

Cora had come without her maid. Henry had
demurred when she spoke of it, and she was
forced to leave her. She had been used to having everything done for her. She had become
accustomed to having the best of everything
going. Above all, she loved her personal com-
fort. She despised personal worry and trouble,
so it was very natural for her to appropriate the
great easy chair which had been provided for
Mother Hunt. She cast her eyes over the
threadbare carpet and the faded curtains. She
quietly kicked an old, well-worn shawl out of
her way, as she took her seat and made some
commonplace remark. In fact, she was still a

little irritated at Pompey's remark about her "paint an' varnish," and was really thinking about some mode of thrashing the boy for his audacity, so she did not hear Mother Hunt's question, asking about "the news in town." However, when it was repeated to her, she gave a very lucid and exact account of her husband's rapid rise in the world, and of her own conquests in society. Her three listeners gave her close attention until she had finished; then Pompey, who had just slipped into the room, saw a ring on her finger, which she had forgotten to remove, and asked: "My goodness, Miss. Cora, is dat ar ring a real diermund?"

"Yes, Pompey, that is a real diamond. Henry paid $2,500 for it for my birthday present, this spring."

"Sholely, den, he can't be so orfully hard up."

"No, he isn't 'hard up' at all. What could have given you such an idea?"

"Den all dem long letters he's been er writin' to Miss Mamie is whoppers, cut clene outen de hole cloff?"

"What on earth does the little ape mean, Mamie?"

"And dat arr $2,500 would er just er paid dat mortgage offer Massa Hunt's farm, too!"

"Come here, Pompey, and get me some wood

to get dinner with," exclaimed Mamie, just at this moment, as she left the room to hide her laughter and her tears, which seemed to be getting mixed. Pompey sprang after his mistress with great alacrity, but he left this parting soliloquy in Cora's ears, as he crossed the room:

"Dat arr man ain't no human at all. He ain't eben er beast. He am worser dan de old debbil hisself."

When Pompey entered the kitchen, he saw the tears in Mamie's eyes, and said: "Miss Mamie, I ain't said nussing to hurt yore feelin's, now, has I?"

"Yes, Pompey. You must not talk this way to my sister again. Please remember that."

"Yessum. I won't say anudder word to her, if you says not ter. You knows I allus minds you."

"That is right. Now take this and go after your wood and water;" and she gave him a bun, which he began to demolish as he went to the wood-pile. After chopping away for a few moments, he stopped and soliloquized as follows: "She needn't ter think that she and her hursben-debbil is er gwyen to spile all uv de happiness of all uv my white fokes, lessen I make it hot fur hur when I gits de chance."

By dint of great patience, the first meal was

gotten over without further trouble, and by this time the position had become less strained, and everybody was feeling more at ease again.

But Cora and Pompey were sworn enemies ever afterwards.

Cora retired early that night. She was tired, and the knowledge of her husband's duplicity, in regard to those mortgages, had made her feel most desolate. She was naturally kind-hearted. She had once loved her parents very dearly, and now that she really understood their situation, she made up her mind to use her best efforts to get Henry to cancel the mortgages. With this in mind, she seated herself and wrote him a long letter, in which she told him the condition of all three of the families. She also gave him an exact description of the condition of the three properties. She wound up this letter with an urgent appeal to him to at once cancel the two mortgages on their parents' farm and return them to her, that she might have the satisfaction of giving them to her parents before she left for New York, which, she announced, would be as soon as she could hear from him on this point.

In due time his reply reached her. He said that it would be impossible for him to comply with her request as to the mortgages until he had conferred with his partner, who was in

Washington; but from the tone of his letter, she decided that Henry would attend to this matter as soon as possible. She showed this letter to her sister and to her mother and mother-in-law, who, believing that Henry's heart had been touched by his wife's appeal, took her to their hearts and blessed the day of her coming to them. Cora then gave them all of the spare money she had with her, which was enough to supply their present needs, and returned home. The good news was written to the poor fathers, who once more felt the rising of hope in their breasts. They also blessed the dear girl, to whom they thought they owed their deliverance.

It is now necessary that the reader should know something about the happenings in the part of the war in which our characters participated. They went out into the Army of Virginia, and had been in many of the hardest-fought battles there, where the greatest battles mankind ever fought were of almost daily occurrence. But while thousands of their comrades had fallen all around them, they had all escaped unharmed. The Confederacy was now doomed. All of its leaders saw this. It was now a matter of the best possible terms of surrender, when General Grant earned the name that must go down the pages of time, forever unique, always revered, and yet comically accurate—the name suggested by the general's well-known initials, U. S., which were then said to stand for Unconditional Surrender Grant. Colonel Hunt's regiment had been with Stonewall Jackson in all of his hardest fights. His men were barefooted, almost naked, poorly fed, and received their pay in Confederate money, which was now worthless. Such was their condition when they surrendered at Appomatox, but with little money and no chance of transportation, these unsung heroes of a lost cause started on their long tramp home, with light hearts and bright hopes. Like old jaded horses, these men marched slowly homeward, in groups and in single file, scattering far and wide on the way. They had to depend upon the charity of the people along their route for something to eat, so that they could not go in large bodies; but Colonel Hunt and his father and father-in-law kept together and walked for many weeks before they reached home. At last they reached home, one night about ten o'clock, and they were worn out, in tatters and half-starved. They almost forgot all of their privations, as they strained their loved ones to their hearts. Supper was soon prepared and "all the news" was discussed, while it was partaken of. No, not all the news, quite. There was one sad item that was carefully passed over, until after the tired soldiers had one good night's sleep.

Next morning, after breakfast, Mamie said to the entire family, now so happily reassembled:

"There is one piece of sad intelligence that we have kept from you until now. But the time has come when we must tell you all. I would have written to you, but I saw it would be too late to reach you, so I have waited until I could tell you in person. We are all homeless."

"Homeless!" exclaimed the three men, rising to their feet simultaneously. "What do you mean?"

"Henry has foreclosed all three of the mortgages."

"Foreclosed the mortgages! Impossible!" exclaimed Father Hunt.

"Husband, it is all too true. Our son Henry has foreclosed the mortgage on our old home, and we are homeless in our old age," said Mother Hunt, as she fell on her husband's neck and wept.

"No son of mine has done this accursed business! Henceforth and forevermore, let his name be a curse. For myself and mine, we shall never again speak the name of such an accursed monster!" and the tall, white-haired old man staggered out of the door, followed by his wife.

"My God! and can this be true?" exclaimed Father Caldwell, as he, too, staggered under this last blow to his hopes. "I thought that Cora had prevailed upon him to cancel the mortgages?"

"So we all thought," answered Mother Caldwell, "but the first thing we knew the farms were all advertised for sale, just a month ago yesterday, when they were sold for considerably less than the mortgage on each of them, and bid in by Henry's agent. We had no money to pay the interest this year, and the farms were advertised the next day after the interest fell due. You all were gone, so we could not consult you, and we went to a lawyer in town, who told us that he saw no way to help us, unless we could pay the mortgages. We then went to the bankers and tried to get them to let us have the money on the farms, but they refused. I do believe that Henry had written to those bankers not to let us have the money; for they did not seem to be surprised at what we told them, and were very curt with their refusal to aid us. In fact, I feel assured that I saw them give a knowing wink at one another, as soon as we entered the bank."

Colonel Hunt had not said a word until now, when he took his wife in his arms, as he said: "For us, my darling, I care but little about this matter. I can make a living for you anywhere. But because of the outrageous injustice done our parents in this matter, I hereby register, before high Heaven, a vow that I will spend my life to gain revenge. Not only shall Henry feel the power of my vengeance, but those in his accursed profession of banking shall answer to me for this high-handed fraud on my parents!"

Here they were called to the door by some one knocking, and when the door opened, the County Sheriff, without ceremony, entered and proceeded as follows:

"I have a very unpleasant duty to perform this morning, ladies and gentlemen, but under an execution from the honorable circuit court of this county, I am instructed to take charge of all the crops, stock, household goods and other property now on this farm, and on the Caldwell farm and on the old Hunt farm, all of which property belongs to you three families; said property to be sold to satisfy a balance still due on certain notes signed by you all and your wives. And I am also instructed to demand immediate possession of all three of those farms, which have been foreclosed under those mortgages."

"Will you allow me to see your papers, sir?" asked Colonel Hunt, as he grasped the full meaning of all the sheriff had said.

"Certainly. Here they are."

After looking over these papers carefully, Colonel Hunt handed them back, saying that he would like to have time to consult an attor-ney. This was readily granted, but with the understanding that the sheriff was to retain pos-session of everything during the delay. Here Pompey was ordered to hitch up the buggy, that Colonel Hunt might drive to town to see an attorney.

"I am very sorry, sir, but my orders are very strict, and I cannot allow you to use anything belonging to the place, in any way. It is my in-tention to lock all the doors at once, and place deputies at each place."

"Do you mean to say that you are going to lock my family out of doors, immediately?"

"My orders are very strict, sir. I am afaird that I will be compelled to insist on absolute possession of everything, at once."

"I suppose that our wearing apparel will not be wanted?"

"I cannot allow you to move one cent's worth of anything. These are my positive orders."

"From whom did you get such inhuman in-structions?"

"From the plaintiff's attorney, who has posi-tive written instructions from New York. I saw the letter written in Henry Hunt's own handwriting, and signed by him."

"Then we have nothing to do but submit. I will take my family to a neighbor's house, while I go to town to see what can be done." And then they all prepared to leave the house, which they did in a few minutes, all talking the matter over in subdued tones.

For the honor of Missouri, be it known that this sheriff was a reconstruction sheriff, and did not belong to the state, in any way.

As our fugitives started away, Pompey begged Colonel Hunt to allow him to stay there, "jist to watch er round a little, yer see." After a moment's reflection, he decided to allow Pompey to stay there to help the sheriff to look after the stock, etc., to which the sheriff readily agreed.

Pompey looked after the retreating figures as long as they were in sight, then he turned to the sheriff and said: "Mister Sherruff, dem's de bestest fokes yer ever seed in yer life."

"Damned rebels, every one of them!" the sheriff answered, more to himself than to the boy.

"Is yer ergin 'em?"

"Who, the rebels? Of course I am."

"Den I specks I knose sumhum yer ort tew know."

"And what is that, my boy?"

"Yer won't giv me erway."

"Of course not. I will protect you if you tell me."

"I knose wharr dar arr a lott uv munney berried."

"Money that belongs to these people?"

"Certain, an' I kin show yer de berry place."

"Then I will pay you well to point it out."

"How much yer gwyen ter giv me?"

"Well, say a third of it. How will that do?"

"An' yer er a-gwyen to keep de rest uv it?"

"Oh, you can trust me to take care of the rest."

"Den it's er go. You jist foller me."

The sheriff followed with alacrity, while Pompey led him into the back yard, near where the smoke-house was standing. He pointed to the farther side of a pile of old rubbish and said: "You ken dig it up rite darr."

The sheriff walked up on top of the pile of rubbish and stooped down and began pulling the brush away with his hand, when, almost before he could think, he found himself falling to the bottom of an old dry well. Pompey had pushed one of the cross-beams, which held the rubbish up, out of place, precipitating the sheriff and the whole pile down fully thirty feet below the surface of the ground. The soft rubbish broke the force of the fall, but the sheriff was badly bruised, when consciousness returned to him, in time to see Pompey's grinning countenance, as he looked down and shouted: "You ken jist dig on threw to Chinar, ole man. De munney what I tole yer about is on de udder side uv de yearth. Yer don't like de rebels, duz yer? Bye-bye!"

CHAPTER VII.

WHEN Colonel Hunt arrived in town, he went directly to the office of Judge Hanna, a famous old attorney, whose upright character and love of justice had long since made him one of the leading attorneys of the state. The judge listened carefully, while the entire matter was laid before him. Then, after consulting a number of law-books, he gave the following opinion:

"In the case of your land, Colonel Hunt, I have but little hope of accomplishing much. We may be able to force them to release the personal property, by giving bond and waiting until our state laws are in force again and then setting up your exemptions, under the statutes. We can do this, at all events; by giving the necessary bonds, we can gain time and put you in possession of your personal property. Your brother's eagerness has caused him to make one mistake, however, in regard to foreclosing all of these mortgages, for this has been done under a Missouri State law, when it should have been done under the instructions of the United States court.

Therefore we have good grounds to set aside the foreclosure on.

"In the case of your father and father-in-law's land we have several good grounds. In the first place, there was really no consideration received for the notes given originally to your brother. In the hands of an innocent party, they would be valid, but in the hands of the man who has profited by this palpable fraud, I feel assured that there is not a jury in the county that would force payment in this summary manner."

Thus it was decided to commence proceedings at once.

In order to get possession of the property immediately, it was necessary that Colonel Hunt should give bonds amounting to about $20,000, but he noticed that when Judge Hanna had completed writing them out, he had signed each one of them himself, unasked. The colonel then placed his own name on each one of them, and taking them in his hand, he started down the street to get more names on them. It was Saturday, and on inquiring, he found that about two hundred of his old army associates were gathered at a hall in some kind of a convention. He made his way into the hall and was greatly surprised to see the entire assembly rise to their feet and give three cheers for Colonel Hunt. He was then borne on the shoulders of four lusty veterans to the platform, where he made a speech which was cheered to the echo. When the convention dismissed, he called two or three of his friends to one side and requested them to sign the bonds for him. One of them took the bonds in his hand, sprang upon the platform and announced that Colonel Hunt wanted to give bonds amounting to $20,000, to gain possession of his own and his father's and his father-in-law's farms again. He called for volunteer signers, and the entire assembly insisted on signing those bonds. And when they were all through, it was found that both the backs and the faces of all three of the bonds were covered with signatures.

The bonds were at once approved, and a deputy marshal was detailed to go with Colonel Hunt to his home, to deliver to the sheriff the order to turn over all of the property to its rightful owners at once.

On arrival at home, Colonel Hunt and the deputy dismounted and went into the house, which they found unlocked. They looked all around for the sheriff, but he was not to be found. Then they went to the barn, but he was not there. Returning to the house, they called loudly for Pompey, who finally answered them, as he was seen coming out of a strip of timber near by. He came sidling along until he was near enough to speak, when he grinned and said: "Golly, Massa Arthur, how you fellers did skeer me!"

"What were you afraid of?"

"I sorter thort dat yer mite be sum more sherruffs."

"What are you afraid of sheriffs for?"

"I was afeard dey mite git *me* dis time."

"Get you for what?"

"I wuz afeard dey mite hang me."

Colonel Hunt decided that it was merely a childish fear that caused the boy to run away and hide himself, so he changed the subject, and asked: "Where is the sheriff that we left here this morning?"

"He's er diggin' arter sum munney dat I tole him erbout."

"What money do you mean?"

"Sum munney what I tole him you all had berried."

"What did he say when you told him this?"

"He promised to give me er third uv it, ef I'd tell."

"And what was he going to do with the rest of it?"

"He said I could trust him to take care of the rest."

"Where is he now?"

"Oh, I's got him safe ernuff.   He can't git erway."

"You've got him?   Got him where?"

"Down in de hole, er diggin' erway, I guess."

"Down in what hole?   Take me to this hole."

"Come dis way, sir.   When I fed de horses, I carried him a cold bisket and tole him not ter hurt hisself er diggin', cause de munney what I told him erbout wuz on de udder side uv de yearth, in Chinar."

"What on earth have you been doing?"

"When you all left dis mornin' I tole him you all wuz de bestest fokes alive. He said yer wuz all damned rebels.   Den I axed him ef he wuz ergin yer, and he said he wuz.   Den I tole him erbout de munney, and put him ter diggin' fur it."

By this time they had reached the edge of the old well, and Pompey stuck his head over it and shouted: "Hows yer likin' de rebels by dis time, Mister Sherruff?"

"Get away from here, you little black devil! Or go and get a rope to get me out of here!" shouted the sheriff, when he heard Pompey's voice.

"Here's sum friends what want ter see yer. Shall I send um down?"

"No, tell them to get me out of here, you devil."

"Is yer found enny munney yit?"

"Get out! Get out! I intend to break every bone in your body, as soon as I get out of here."

"Not ez long ez my legs can pack me erway, you won't."

Colonel Hunt and the deputy marshal had been convulsed with laughter, until this moment; but now they interfered, and set about getting the sheriff out, which they finally accomplished, after considerable trouble.

"Where is that little devil? Let me at him."

"You don't like rebels, does yer, Mister Sheriff?" shouted Pompey, as he disappeared in the woods.

We must now go back a few years in order to bring up the history of our characters in New York. The reader will remember that Cora Hunt had just returned from her visit to see her parents, declaring that she would do all in her power to get Henry to cancel the mortgages on their parents' farm. She complied with her promise, as far as she was able, but she could not induce Henry to cancel these mortgages. She found that he had but one god, and that it was Gold. But it was to her influence the two extensions were due. She also sent home many presents to her parents and sister, during the trying times of the last two years of the war.

On his return, after spending one year in Washington, Mr. Lyman held the following conversation with Henry:

"We have accomplished a great deal this year; but it has been very difficult, and very expensive. We succeeded in getting the Secretary of the Treasury to recommend the issuance of the bonds, and finally secured the passage of the necessary law; but not until the President had issued his famous Treasury Notes. These are going to worry us a great deal. We cannot corner them, nor can we control them. The people are glad to get them, are anxious to keep them, and I fear they will be hard to destroy. However, I succeeded in getting in the clause, making them money for all purposes except for the payment of duties on imports and interest on the public debt. This will finally have a tendency to depreciate them. Now, if we can only succeed in getting in one more clause, making them payable in gold, or even in coin, it will be a great point gained."

"Yes," answered Henry, "you have done well. I feel assured that if we can get a clause in, making these Treasury Notes payable in coin, that will answer; for we bankers will have but little trouble to convince the Secretary of the Treasury that, if he pays them in silver, gold will immediately go to a premium. And if he does, we can easily carry gold up to a premium, for we have an almost certain corner on gold, any time we want to use it. That much is certain."

"Yes, certainly, we are safe on that proposition. Now, Henry, I want to make my report. My account shows that I have saved just $125,-000 for us, out of the lobby funds. I have carried every point I was expected to carry, and my relatives in England are so well pleased with my work that they have written me to pass the rest of their funds to my credit, to pay me for my own time and trouble in this matter. Here is a check for your half of it. Now let me hear what you have done."

"You have done exceedingly well, Mr. Lyman, exceedingly well. Still, I do not feel that I should be ashamed of my year's work, either."

"Well, what are our average deposits?"

"About $1,350,000."

"And our average loans and discounts?"

"A little over one million dollars, at ten per cent."

"Then, the short-time brokerage?"

"Shows a net profit of $25,000, over all expenses."

"Hadn't we better increase our capital stock to, say, $250,000?"

"I think so, decidedly."

"And what about our salaries?"

"Well, let me see. Profits on loans and discounts, $100,000; on short-time brokerage, $25,-000; total, $125,000. Then $25,000 will pay us ten per cent dividends on $250,000 capital stock, leaving just $100,000 for salaries. I see that our salaries will need to be $50,000 per annum, sir, unless we want to run our dividends up too high for comfort. Let me see, $50,000 salary each, per annum, is as much as the president of the United States receives, and the pretty part of it is, that ours comes to us entirely clear of all expenses, while the president of the United States has to spend most of his salary on expensive state dinners, and the like, and be at the beck and call of every Tom, Dick and Harry who happens to want a favor, at the same time."

"Yes," answered Mr. Lyman, complacently, "this beats being president of the United States, even though he does get $50,000 per annum. You see, every year will increase our income, while the position of the president will become more irksome every year, with additional cost, while the longer we run our bank, the better able to run it will our help become. Yes, Henry, this beats being president all hollow. Let me congratulate you, my boy."

"It is I who should congratulate you, and thank you for all of your goodness to me, Mr. Lyman; for it has been your guiding hand that has enabled me to be what I am. Let me congratulate you."

"This is the proudest homage that you could render me, Henry. It proves that I have made a success in life, in my chosen calling. It proves to me that my head was level when I chose you for a partner. I hope that we may live long to enjoy each other's friendship."

CHAPTER VIII.

ONE year later, when Mr. Lyman and Henry met in their "annual stockholders' meeting," the former rubbed his hands together gleefully, as he exclaimed: "Henry, you must go down to Washington with me to-morrow. I want to introduce you to our Queen of the Lobby. Ah! that was a happy thought of mine. Few men can resist a really smart, pretty woman's influence. Knowing this, I employed the Countess Ilman, who has been engaged in this lobby work in Europe, to come to my aid. And the result has been most satisfactory, in every way. You would laugh yourself to death if you could see how she handles our Congressmen—especially those just arrived from the green country districts. We are maintaining a magnificent establishment for her, where she receives and is received by all of the best families in Congress. When one of our new Congressmen arrives, we secure an introduction for her and she takes him in charge. Of course, he has come to Washington full of great reforms for the benefit of the people. He is just bubbling over with patriotism, with the 'Give me liberty, or give me death' idea in it. In a few visits, the Countess succeeds in finding out how he stands on all of our schemes, and reports to us. If he is really a dangerous man to us, of course we are forced to buy him off. And this is done in a hundred different ways. Some of these old country greenhorns are absolutely unpurchasable, but we find that most of the Congressmen from the large cities are easily handled. They are in for the money. They have obtained their offices by fraud, or by the use of money, and they expect to make money out of them.

"It is very amusing to see how she manages some of those patriots. Many of them change their views because she has laughed at them as foolish; some, because she asks it as a personal favor; others, because she has made love to them and influences them in that way; quite a number change because she convinces them that their scheme is impracticable, and will make them the laughing-stock of the entire country—ah, that is a great dodge!—a few, the wily old politicians from the cities, demand so much money, which we pay promptly, if the measure is of sufficient importance. There is now a very strong railroad lobby at Washington, so we have joined hands with them that we may absolutely control all legislation that we desire to control. Their interests and ours are practically identical. They want *cheap labor*; we want *dear money*, which amounts to the same in effect. And for the first time I feel secure. We have proven that we can defeat any measure that we desire to defeat. I shall soon demonstrate the fact that I can carry any measure that I want to pass. The bankers of the United States are at last becoming thoroughly organized. They are working together like beavers. Every bank on our lists has paid every assessment made, this year. I am educating them. It will not be long before every banker in the land will know more about the real secrets of banking than the president of the United States does. By the bye, it would be a good idea to put a banker into the White House and another in as Secretary of the Treasury. I will start that ball to rolling, anyway. And now, to business. Here is a check for your part of my wages, which have been increased again this year."

"Do you mean to say that my part of your wages is $125,000?" asked Henry, in astonishment.

"Certainly. You see the check."

"Then let me congratulate you on your success."

"And how about your progress?"

"Oh, I have done fairly well, myself."

"What have been our average deposits this year?"

"About $2,750,000."

"Loans and discounts?"

"About $2,500,000, at ten per cent per annum."

"Short-time brokerage?"

"About $50,000 above all expenses."

"Ah, ha, Henry, I see you have beaten me this year!"

"Yes, but then, you see, I had the entire bank to operate on, while you were single-handed."

"Quite right, in one sense; but you must remember that I have handled a great deal more money than you have. I must raise my assessments. It will never do to allow you to beat me in this way. Let me congratulate you on your wonderful success."

"Yes, sir, I consider that $300,000 profit, on a capital of only $250,000, is pretty good results in one year's time. It is good banking, at all events."

"So it is, my boy, so it is. And now, what have our private enterprises done? You know that I turned mine over to you, last year."

"They seem to have stopped at the old figures again."

"What, only $50,000 each again, this year!"

"That is all, sir."

"Then we must turn them into diamond brokerage establishments. I have a cousin who thoroughly understands diamond brokerage, so I will write to England for him to come at once. We cannot afford to waste our time on a slow business, like the pawn business seems to have turned out to be. We must have results. Now, about the bank capital. Hadn't we better increase it to $500,000?"

"I think so, decidedly."

"So let it be. What about salaries, Henry?"

"We will have to make our salaries $150,000 each per annum, in order to keep the dividends down."

"Certainly. That is right. And now, Henry, what about being president of the United States? Do you feel like you want to change places with him?"

"A man would be a fool if he resigned such positions as we now hold, to be president of the United States. No sensible man would give up a position that was paying him $150,000 per annum, all clear profit, with the chance of doubling this salary in the future, to take a measly president's chair, at $50,000 salary per annum, and have to pay his living expenses out of that."

"In my opinion, a man would be a fool if he did not make millions out of one term of the presidency. I stand ready to pay the money to the first president who will do as I dictate to him. Yes, sir, millions!"

"Then, sir, you will soon find your man. Never fear."

"Oh, I know that. We have matters just as we want them. The game is coming our way. All that we need to do now, is to catch it as it comes. There is only one more hard knot to unravel, and that is the question of those Treasury Notes, which we must destroy. We must get rid of that greenback money. It is absolutely necessary that it should be called in and destroyed. The people cling onto it with peculiar pertinacity. They actually prefer it to gold. I am just now starting in on a general crusade against it, and here is the first gun of the campaign. Read it."

Mr. Lyman then handed a circular to Henry, who read:

"Dear Sir:—It is advisable to do all in your power to sustain such prominent daily and weekly papers, *especially the agricultural and religious press, as will oppose the issuing of greenback paper money,* and that you also withhold patronage of favors from all applicants who *are not* willing to oppose the governmental issue

of money.   Let the government issue the coin
and the banks issue the paper money, *for then
we can better protect each other*.   To repeal the
law creating National Bank Notes, or to restore
to circulation the governmental issue of money,
will be to provide the people with money, and
will, therefore, *seriously affect your individual
profit* AS BANKERS AND LENDERS. *See your congressman at once, and engage him to support
our interests, that we may control legislation.*"

"I propose," said Mr. Lyman, when Henry
had finished reading the circular, "to have this
circular signed by our American Bankers' Association, and then send it to every bank on our
lists."

"But is it not very dangerous?   If the public
should happen to get hold of one of these circulars, would there not be a great roar against the
banks?"

"There certainly would.   But we would be
able to deny out of it.   We could have every
banker in the land deny any knowledge of such
a circular, or even of such an association.   Be-
sides, there is very little chance of its getting
out.   It will be sent out confidentially, to none
but our own tried and true friends, whose interests will make them very careful. Then, it
is one of the main objects of this circular to put
a muzzle on the press.   The managers of the

great dailies could not be persuaded to publish that circular. They know that they cannot exist without the banker's influence. They know that it would be financial suicide for them to attempt to oppose the banker's influence. I tell you, we are getting a pretty firm hold on the people of this government already, and in ten years more we expect to make it a perfect sinch. Do you know that all the governments of Europe belong to the bankers, now; that no country can afford to go to war without the consent of the money-kings, who always insist on getting some great concession before they will agree to the war? Such is the fact, and we are fast getting this government in the same shape.

"The great secret of the bankers' success seems to have escaped the sages and savants of all countries. These so-called patriots have never had sense enough to know that the people are entitled to the use of their own money, made by their own governments, without interest or charge of any kind; and that the bankers have so manipulated matters that really all of the money belonging to the people, except a small margin kept on hand by the banker for safety, is now drawing interest all the time; which interest goes directly into the bankers' vaults, as clear profit, while it ought to be turned into the credit of each and every depositor of the bank, according to the amount he has on deposit in the bank at the time. Thus, you see, the people are forced to pay the banker interest on their own money; for all men are borrowers, as well as depositors, and all are caught in our net."

"You are right, sir," answered Henry, "we have a 'sure thing' game, with all the world as our victims. Our only danger lies in bad loans."

"A banker is a fool if he lets out one dollar where there is a shadow of a show of losing it. Now, just for our own satisfaction, tell me how much we have lost since you have been with this bank?"

"There have been no absolute losses, but we have several thousand dollars' worth of unfinished business."

"What does it consist of?"

"I am sorry to say that most of it is charged up to my own relatives. I have done my best to collect those notes, but have never been able to do so, without foreclosing the mortgages. This would have been unpleasant to my wife and I, because there would have been a great howl over it. But I have decided to do it, let the result be what it may. I did not take charge of this bank to allow it to be beat out of its money, especially by my own relatives. I shall forward all of the papers in these three cases to an attorney this evening, with strict instructions to foreclose."

"What is the total amount, and what is it for?"

"Why, you remember that my father gave his note for $2,500, and my father-in-law gave his note for $2,500, when I first went into the bank. Then, in order to get these notes secured on each of their farms, which were well worth $10,000 each, I was forced to carry a $4,000 mortgage on my brother's farm, which was also well worth $10,000. This gives me an investment of $9,000 well secured on $30,000 worth of choice Missouri farms."

"Have they paid the interest promptly?"

"Oh, yes, I would have foreclosed them long since, if they had not done so. You can bet I looked after that! I even made them pay the last interest in advance before I would make the extension, which was applied for by a lot of the neighbors, who seem to think that it is their duty to meddle with my affairs."

"The two old men really received nothing when they signed those notes, did they?"

"N-no, but they signed them as part of my part of their estates, and they should have paid them."

"I believe I would cancel the mortgages on

the two old homesteads, if I were you, Henry, and send them to your own and your wife's parents, to celebrate the fact of our wonderful success. You can mark the amounts up to 'profit and loss.'"

"But, my dear friend, do you think I would permit you to lose one cent through my relatives? If there is to be a loss, then it is mine. But there is really no reason why I should allow them to beat me out of a lot of money, and cause me to break one of the strongest rules of my life, through my sympathies. A banker has no business with sympathies. I do not care for the money. It is the principle at stake. I intend to force them to pay every cent of those debts at once, and will write out the instructions this very evening."

"Have your own way, my boy, have your own way."

But Mr. Lyman found himself thinking about it when he reached his own rooms. "It was a heartless thing to do," he soliloquized, "but I suppose that Henry is right about not having any sympathies, as a banker. Such things are well enough for common people. Still, I have half a mind to send a check to pay it off, myself, but I suppose I had better not do so."

CHAPTER IX.

COLONEL HUNT and his father and father-in-law went to work with a will. It was not long before they had all of their farms blossoming like a rose. It was very hard work, but each of them felt that their only salvation depended on getting a big crop during the delay in the trial of their cases, and they worked like beavers. It is true that they were short of even the necessities of life; but they drank "potato coffee," without sugar, had meat once a day, and ate vegetables, bread, milk and butter, and throve upon it. Their good wives took their places behind the old-fashioned looms, and long ere the winter days arrived, had plenty of clothing for all of the family. It was too late to plant a crop of corn, but every acre of their land was sown in wheat that fall, and thanks to a merciful Providence, they gathered a bountiful harvest in the spring. Prices of wheat were very high the next fall, and when the cases were finally brought up for trial, each one of them had about $1,000 cash in hand to apply on the debts. This was duly reported to Henry, who at once instructed his agent to accept these amounts and extend the rest one year, provided all the expenses were paid by the defendants. Accordingly this was done, and the farms were once more planted in wheat.

Henry's name was never mentioned among them. No communications of any kind were had with him or his wife, except through the attorneys. They had all made up their minds to pay off the mortgages, as fast as possible, and they were doing so with a will.

However, hard as Colonel Hunt was working, he was reading and studying still harder. He had managed to get a vast lot of information in regard to the plans and policies of the national banks. He reviewed the actions of both of the great parties regarding our banking laws, and found that neither of them had ever been, in practice, opposed to anything the bankers demanded. He saw that not only Congress, but even the state legislatures, passed all laws that were favored by the banks. He noted the fact that very few of the great papers had the temerity to oppose any measure that was being vigorously advocated by the banks. He then examined the details of banking, and very soon ran up on a query that staggered him: "Why on earth

do all of the people give the banks the use of all
of their money all the time, free of charge, and
then so readily agree to pay the banks an
exorbitant interest, if they happen to want to
borrow a little money from the banks?"

This query was with him all the time. He
could not get rid of the idea. What in the world
did the people mean? Were they all fools? He
thought of the billions of dollars that were de-
posited in the banks all the time. "No wonder
the bankers are getting rich," he exclaimed to
himself, "when the people give them the use of
all of their own money free of charge, and then
pay the banks for every cent they happen to
need themselves! Why, the bankers are really
getting interest on all of the money in the country, nearly, while most of it belongs to the very
people who are, at various times, borrowing it!
In effect, this amounts to the people borrowing
from themselves, and paying the banker the interest! My God! What folly! It will bank-
rupt every man in the country, except the bankers, who are bound to grow immensely rich!"

Thus he reasoned, as he plowed his wheat
land. In this way his mind was employed as
he gathered in his harvest. During his leisure
hours he read every book he could obtain on
finance and banking. So it was that he learned,

that from time immemorial, the money-lord
tries to keep the poor producer in ignorance of
the manner in which he is being robbed, that
the robber might continue his rascality. And
yet it is such a simple matter. "Why," he soliloquized, "do the business men submit to such
an outrage? Why don't they combine, start a
bank of their own, elect one of their number
manager, loan their own deposits and get the
interest themselves? The bankers are no wiser
than the business men, except on this point.
Any good sensible man can run a bank, after
he studies it a little. Why, look at the men right
here among us, who have become bankers.
They are no smarter than hundreds of their
neighbors. And yet they go on and get rich,
and no one seems to ask the reason of it. They
get rich, while the poor business man and farmer
gets poorer and poorer, or else struggles along
to hold his own, and still nobody tries to inquire
the reason why it is so!"

Colonel Hunt was not very reticent with open
expressions of these thoughts, and they soon had
others thinking a little on their own account.
These expressions soon gave him the reputation
of being a far-seeing man. His neighbors spoke
of him as a coming man. They all looked upon
him as an honest, fearless patriot.

Mr. Lyman produced a check for $200,000 as Henry's share in his next year's work, at the next stockholders' meeting, and then asked, as usual:

"What are our average deposits, Henry?"

"About $4,000,000."

"Loans and discounts?"

"About $3,650,000, at 9 per cent per annum."

"Short-time brokerage?"

"About $75,000 above all expenses."

"Ah, Henry, I see we are about even this time. We have each added about $400,000 to our capital this year."

"But there is the diamond brokerage, sir."

"So there is. I will be bound that you will beat me again. How has my cousin turned out?"

"Very well, I suppose, although he declares that he is just getting the business under headway."

"What are his profits, so far?"

"A little over $100,000 at each place, $200,-000 in all."

"Ah!" exclaimed Mr. Lyman, "that makes a little over a million dollars clear profits this year. Pretty good, my dear boy. Allow me to congratulate you."

"Allow me to return the congratulations, with my best wishes for your continued good health and happiness." And they shook hands heartily.

"But I have two points for congratulations yet."

"Name them, my dear boy, name them," said Mr. Lyman.

"First, I have collected $1,500 on my brother's mortgage, and $1,000 each from my father and father-in-law. This makes these investments absolutely safe, and as they are paying me ten per cent interest, while I find that it is hard to average nine per cent here, I have offered to extend them indefinitely. This relieves me from the stain of my relatives disgracing themselves, and the bank from the stain of losing anything."

"Never mind about telling me this—I mean, that it is all right—you know best, at all events," said Mr. Lyman, rising to leave the room.

"But, wait!" exclaimed Henry, at a loss to account for the strange conduct of his partner, "you have not heard my best news yet."

"Well, what is it?" rather gruffly.

"I have a son and heir," blushing like a boy.

"Glad to know it, sir, glad to know it. But I must really be going now." He then retired to the corridor, where he said to himself: "I wish he would never mention those accursed mortgages to me again. It was a beastly thing to do, and I cannot help but shudder, while he is continually calling my attention to them!"

Henry was puzzled. After studying about the matter for some time, he said: "I have it. He told me to cancel those two mortgages on the old homesteads of my father and father-in-law, last year, and I did not do it. This has offended him. I will cancel them and send them to the old people this very evening. Yes, I will send Arthur his, too, with a letter, telling about the little one."

An hour later he mailed his letter, with the first glow of real human feeling that he had felt in years. He had become a machine, which was incapable of enjoying any emotions save the greed of gain. But the coming of his little son opened up his heart a little. And he kissed his wife when he reached home. And she was very much surprised, and wept.

That night, Cora surprised Henry by asking him to let her "go home" for a month or two. At first he would not listen to the idea, but she insisted, and finally he gave his consent. Baby was now six weeks old, and Henry could not make this an excuse to keep her, so he sent her away, with a strange feeling at his heart.

Cora drove up to her mother's door in a hired vehicle, unannounced. She was alone, so she hitched the horse, took baby in her arms and walked into her mother's room, which she found unoccupied. She heard a noise in a back room, so she laid baby on the bed and went quietly into this room, where she found her mother weaving lustily. Almost before Mother Caldwell could utter a word, Cora had her arms around her neck and was weeping, as she pleaded: "Mother, my heart is broken! Won't you love me again? Oh, how my heart hungers for love! I have been loveless for ten long years. I cannot stand it any longer. What care I for all the pomp and vanities of the world, if I cannot have some one to love? Oh, mother! Please don't look at me that way! Scold me! Beat me, if you will, but, oh, love me again! Take me to your heart again. I know what you feel. I cannot excuse my conduct, but, oh, let me love you again."

Mother Caldwell's face was a study. Pride, outraged love, resentment and bitterness were all striving for the mastery. Her arms had dropped down by her sides, and were encircled by those of Cora, whose streaming eyes and disheveled hair were directly in front of her.

But unluckily for poor Cora, a discussion had been held over the receipt of those canceled mortgages by all interested parties, only the night before, and it had been agreed, unanimously, that they should be returned to Henry, with the haughty intelligence that they would be paid in full. They had been demanded at a time when payment was impossible, but now that it would be possible to pay them so soon, it would not be possible for them to allow of any discount being taken off. They would be paid to the last cent. During this consultation, Mother Caldwell had sworn that no daughter of hers would live with a man who had made his money by such methods. She remembered all this as Cora was pleading, and when she had ceased, her mother rose, pushed her back from her and said: "You are no longer my daughter! Why have you come here to mock me in this way? You are a pretty daughter, dressed up in your finery, wearing your diamonds, while your old gray-haired mother is running a loom for a living!" With this, Mother Caldwell started to go into her own room, dragging her weeping daughter with her. The unusual noise had awakened the baby, and he began to cry. In one moment Cora had the child in her arms, her own tears streaming into his face, as she exclaimed: "Mother, can't you see that it is baby who has done it? Baby has changed my heart! Baby's coming has shown me how mean I have been to you! Mother, can't you forgive me for baby's sake?"

"My God! This is more than I can bear!". she exclaimed, as she fell back into her easy chair.

Cora laid the child in her mother's lap, as she knelt at her knees. Baby seemed to think that it was all right again, so he began looking at his grandmother with eyes wide open with astonishment.

"God bless the child! It has done one good deed already, if it has put you to thinking!" exclaimed Mother Caldwell, as she pressed the little one to her heart. This seemed. to break the ice, and she poured into Cora's ears a stream of heart-longings, heart-aches and unhappiness, for an hour or more, while Cora wept on her knee. She wound up the proceeding by giving her daughter a good kissing, a hearty hugging, and thanking her Creator for restoring her long-lost daughter to her arms again. Then she suddenly remembered that it was getting late and that she had to get some supper and that she "didn't know what on earth she would cook for that baby to eat."

"Why, mother, baby can't eat anything. He nurses."

"Of course he does, bless his little heart. But I don't know what your father will say, and I don't know what everybody will say, but I don't care. If you are going to treat me as a daughter should, then I ain't the mother to keep you from doing your duty."

"Now, that's my darling old mother, herself again," exclaimed Cora, as the kissing scene began again.

Cora had on an old apron and was busy helping her mother in the kitchen, when her father came in from work. When he had been told all that had taken place, he said: "I knew your mother couldn't hold out long, when she saw that baby. By the bye, where is the young man? I would like to see my first grandson once, myself."

And so baby was exhibited to his delighted grandfather, and all four were happier than they had been for many a day.

Cora's visit was uneventful after this. Her father and mother took her to their hearts again, but she did not expect to be very well received by Colonel Hunt, or his family or friends. They treated her kindly, but she could see there was little real cordiality in their manner. Mamie seemed to be much the prouder of the two sisters. She had condemned the heartlessness of Henry so bitterly that she could not overcome her repugnance at seeing Henry's wife and child. However, Mother and Father Hunt received her very cordially. They knew Henry, and blamed him for his heartlessness to them, but they did not have the heart to condemn his wife and innocent baby, on his account. Yet there was one point that all parties drew the line at. Not one of them all would accept a single present from Cora. Mother Caldwell took the lead in this, when Cora wanted to get her some better furniture and carpets. "No, Cora," she had said, "I cannot accept anything from your husband. It would seem to me like blood money, for I know that he has cheated some poor mortal out of it."

"Oh, mother, don't talk that way," said Cora.

"I must do it, child. Every mortgage that he has foreclosed has robbed some poor family out of a home. He has not earned a single dollar of all that vast fortune that he has gained. By some hook or crook in the law, he has wrenched it out of the shriveled hand of labor; has gathered it in away from some deserving person. See what wretchedness he tried to bring upon his own parents! Would an honorable man have done that? Would an honest man take such a mean advantage of any one, as to get them to sign a note for his own accommodation, and then take that same note and sell his friend out of house and home? No, Cora, if you ever need a friend, or a home, or anything that we can do

for you, come to us; but do not expect us to
receive your husband, or any of his ill-gotten
gains."

And with this decision Cora was forced to be
content, and after a month's visit she returned
to New York, feeling that she was leaving all
that was worth living for behind her.

The wheat crop was a failure this year, so it
was found that it would be impossible for them
to pay anything on the principal of the mortgages, but interest in full was mailed to Henry
by the attorney, and was promptly thrown into
the fire by him, no answer being vouchsafed.
When the mortgages were returned to him, he
had treated them in the same way, swearing that
he would never write them another line, as he did
so. He had burned up the mortgages, but he could
not eradicate the words of his brother's manly
letter from his memory. They were burned
into living letters of fire on his heart, and he
could not forget them. He saw them yet; he
could read them now:—

"At the request of our parents, I herewith return to you the mortgages that your greed for
gain has wrenched from their aged, trembling
hands, with the assurance that they will pay
them just as soon as possible. After accepting
the pitiful earnings of your own mother, of your
own mother-in-law and of your sister-in-law,

during all of the four years of our civil war, as
interest on those accursed mortgages,while their
husbands were away in the war, you cannot now
refuse to accept both principal and interest from
those husbands,who insist on paying every cent
covered in your unholy demand.

"But this is not all. After persuading your
father and father-in-law to sign two accommodation notes to enable you to get into business,
which has made you the real owner, or half-
owner of these notes, and then insisting on a
mortgage on their homesteads to secure these
notes, on which mortgages you absolutely attempted to foreclose those homesteads, when
you knew that their owners were away and that
their wives were widows, at the time, you cannot now refuse to accept payment in full, when
it is tendered to you. In the hope that all of
these facts may enter your heart as a blade of
steel, and that they may produce suitable effects,
I am, etc."

"Confound that accursed letter! I wish I
could get it out of my mind. I wish I had sent
them those mortgages when Lyman told me that
I had better send them, for then, perhaps, they
would have accepted them. Now I shall never
hear the last of them. Damn that interest money
that they have just sent me! I wouldn't touch
a cent of it for a kingdom. I'll burn the whole
thing up!" So saying, he threw the letter,
check and all, into the fire and watched them
burn up into ashes.

"I wonder what is coming over me, anyway!" he soliloquized. "I am getting as nervous as a rat. It seems to me that people are avoiding me. Even my wife shivers, if I happen to touch her, just as though she had been touched by a viper. God! It's fearful!"

Once more the annual stockholders' meeting is in session. "My profits have been $500,000," said Lyman.

"I have an anomalous state of affairs," said Henry. "In the first place, we forgot to vote ourselves any salary at the last meeting. In the next place, we neglected to make any arrangements about our profits at that meeting, so that I have been carrying $1,000,000 as a surplus, with only $500,000 capital stock, this year."

"You have not advertised this surplus, have you?"

"No, I have not."

"Then it is easily settled. What are our average deposits?"

"About $6,500,000."

"Loans and discounts?"

"About $6,250,000, at 8 per cent per annum."

"Short-time brokerage?"

"About $300,000, above all expenses."

"Diamond brokerage?"

"About $300,000 clear profits."

"That is $1,600,000 clear profits, $800,000 each. How does that compare with the salary of the president of the United States, eh, Henry?"

"Eight hundred thousand dollars each, clear profits, in one year! It seems almost incredible!" said Henry.

"But there are the figures to prove it, Henry."

"I know it, sir; there is no doubt about it."

"I guess we had better increase the capital stock of the bank to $3,000,000, hadn't we, Henry?"

"I think so, decidedly."

"And our salaries?"

"The bank cleared over $800,000 clear profits."

"And will beat that badly next year."

"Then I think we might vote ourselves a salary of $500,000 each, this next year, to make up for not getting any salary this year, don't you?"

"I think so, decidedly, sir."

"But we must remember that we will have to declare a dividend on $3,000,000 capital stock next year, instead of on a measly $500,000 of this year."

"That is so. Quite a rise, isn't it? But then, I think there will be plenty of money, even for that."

"There is no doubt of it, sir."

"Henry, I have a scheme."

"What is it, sir?"

"I am compelled to keep more or less money in Washington all the time, anyway. Why not take, say about $100,000 down there and start a branch bank?"

"That is a capital idea."

"Then I will do that, when I return."

"You can take down some of the boys from here to aid."

"So I was thinking. They understand our methods."

"Certainly, and can train others to help them."

"This has been rather a quiet year for the lobby. We killed several bills and passed two or three. But our best work has been done on the press. Yes, sir, we have accomplished great results on the papers. You could not get a corporal's guard out of all of the great dailies, that would oppose any measure that we advocate. I have reports from all of our banks, and I am glad to see that they are taking such a prominent stand in politics. And they are electing our men, everywhere. In a few years we will be able to call in the greenbacks and demonetize silver. Yes, sir, everything is coming our way, and easily, at that."

CHAPTER X.

THE reconstruction of Missouri had been completed and it had once more taken its place under the Stars and Stripes. Candidates were being announced for the various offices, and politicians had begun engineering their various schemes. With one accord, his old soldiers turned to Colonel Hunt to make the race for Congress. He was the unanimous choice of the Democratic party, and his nomination was accomplished with a whoop. His great personal popularity, his unswerving honesty, his well-known integrity and his unsurpassed eloquence made him a strong candidate, but he found that the opposition was very strong. Money was being used freely in the attempt to elect a young banker, who had been chosen by the Republican party, as their candidate to Congress. This banker had applied to Mr. Lyman for aid, and that gentleman, remembering Henry's cruelty to his family, had promptly refused to advance a single cent. He was rather rejoiced to see Henry's brother rising to be of some consequence in his district, and would have gladly donated something to aid him and his cause, had the chance of doing so appeared to him. Mr. Lyman had no politics. He was all things to all men. But perhaps the only circumstance that had ever worked on his sympathies was Henry's cruelty to his relatives. He felt so safe in his position, as leader of the lobby for the bankers, that he decided that one congressman could not do him much harm, and therefore he was anxious to see Colonel Hunt elected. These were the circumstances, when Mr. Lyman went to New York to attend the next "annual stock-holders' meeting" of the two banks.

"Well, how does the new bank flourish?" asked Henry.

"Oh, I guess we are doing very well."

"What are your average deposits?"

"About $350,000?"

"Pretty good for the first year. And loans?"

"About $300,000, at 8 per cent per annum."

"Short-time brokerage?"

"Paid all expenses."

"Lobby profits?"

"About $500,000."

"That makes about $525,000 clear profits."

"Yes. What are our average deposits in New York?"

"About $10,000,000."

"Loans and discounts?"

"About $9,750,000, at 8 per cent per annum."

"Short-time brokerage?"

"Paid $400,000 above all expenses of the bank."

"Diamond brokerage?"

"About $400,000 clear profits, this year."

"Ah, then your total profits are $1,580,000 this year."

"Which, added to your profits, makes over $2,000,000."

"Yes, Henry, we have made over $1,000,000 apiece."

"A pretty good year's work, I should say!"

"Especially when we only work six hours per day!"

"And not very hard work at that," laughing.

"Ah, Henry, how does that compare with being president?"

"Pshaw! That beats being king of England!"

"Yes, for we have no worries whatever."

"You are right, sir, you are right."

After increasing the capital stock of the New York bank to $5,000,000, agreeing on a salary of $750,000 each for that bank, and of $10,000 each for the bank at Washington, Mr. Lyman said: "Oh, yes, I wanted to tell you some good news, myself. I am to be married to the Countess Ilman, during the holidays of Congress, and would like to have you bring your family down."

"Certainly. Allow me to congratulate you."

"And I expect you will meet your brother there."

"Meet my brother at your wedding! What do you mean?"

"He will be elected to Congress next month, and I expect to invite him to come to my wedding. I want to get acquainted with him. He has quite taken my fancy, and as the lobby will have such a large majority in the next Congress, I have not opposed your brother's election, although they tell me he is one of the strongest 'Anti-bankers' in the country."

Henry was bewildered, and for an hour or more he remained in his seat studying the matter over. "Arthur in Congress!" he soliloquized. "What on earth does he want to go to Congress for? Who on earth is sending him? Oh, I know him! He hates me and wants a chance to work against me at Washington! He intends to try to pass a law against the bankers, just because I am one of them! There is no turning him, and he will soon be popular. He always was popular. Everybody always likes him. What shall I do? I know. I will defeat him. I will go down there in person and help defeat him. Money will do anything. I'm off to-morrow."

It was still three weeks to the election, when Henry arrived, but he was soon closeted with the Republican leaders, who had out their bands and were marching the streets that very night. Henry stopped at a hotel in town, and did not attempt to see any of his relatives. He had business on hand and he was attending to it. He used money freely and carried everything before him. The managers of his party were enthusiastic and his strikers were hard at work. Every man who could make a speech in public, favoring the Republicans, found himself with a brass band at his command, and plenty of shouters to cheer him at every point.

Colonel Hunt was depressed. Not so much at the idea of defeat, as at the methods that were at work to defeat him. He said nothing about his brother, in his speeches, but he exposed the methods of the opposition mercilessly. He found that he had gathered about him all of the prominent men in his district, but it looked very much as though the rabble would be able to outvote his friends. The real animus of the fight was soon discovered. The people understood the reason why Henry was making such a desperate fight against his own brother, and many

of the leading Republicans at once advocated
Colonel Hunt's election. Every speech he made
won him friends. Every attack on him by
Henry caused some thinking man to come over
to his side. But Henry was spending money
freely. He was a consummate manager, and
everything possible was done and well done.
Election day and its fights, broils and bitterness
came and passed at last, and it was found that
Colonel Hunt had been elected by a small majority.

Henry had spent $100,000 and was defeated,
and he left town for New York, while the guns
were celebrating his brother's victory.

Colonel Hunt's entrance into Congress was
uneventful. He began studying the situation he
found himself in with great interest. Here he
found the hardest problem he had yet met with.
It was a stupendous affair. He was certain of
that. It seemed to him that every action of
Congress was wrapped in such a cloak of rules
and regulations, as to utterly befuddle the brain
of ordinary people. He saw members fighting
over minor rules and precedents, instead of
really trying to pass any legislation of any kind.
He found that here the game of politics became
a science. Here, men consulted the interest of
their political party, instead of the interests of

the whole people.   To him it seemed that Congress was being used to further the interest of
its members, rather than the interests of the people who had to pay the bills.   He saw measures
passed with a wink and a nod.   He soon saw
that there was an outside influence at work.   He
made up his mind to ferret this influence out
and see who and what was at the back of it.
He said but little, but took note of everything
that was done.   After a time he became aware
of the fact that every measure that was really
passed, almost, was one that favored the money-
lords, the bankers or the railroads.

Colonel Hunt was surprised to find his name
mentioned as one of the members of the Committee on Finance and Banking, and he won-
dered who, or what influence had placed it there.
It was the one committee that he really desired
to get on, and he felt very much gratified to find
that he had secured the place so easily.   At the
first meeting of the committee, he made the acquaintance of all the members and began a careful study of their characters.   He readily decided
that there were part of them open, fair, honest
men, but he was not so sure about the rest.   In
fact, he felt sure that some of them were the paid
instruments of the banks.   He found that a recommendation from a banker was more respected

than one from the president. He found that a letter from a banker was given more attention than a petition singed by a thousand good citizens. It had appeared to him that it would be a good idea for him to go slow and be careful that he understood the situation before he took a stand in any way, so he acted on this idea, and found it a good one. He soon found that he was respected by the members of his committee, because he seldom took a wrong stand, and readily changed his views if he found that he was wrong. But this committee soon found that he was as firm as a rock, once he became assured that he was right.

The first two weeks of Congress had passed and he was beginning to feel at home in his new position, when one evening, just as he and another member of the committee were leaving the committee room, he was introduced to Mr. Lyman, whom he found to be a gentleman of the most pleasing manners he had yet met. He had no idea that this was his brother's partner, nor did he dream that he was the manager of the lobby. The two men looked each other over, talked a few minutes and parted with the expression that they might meet again. And on the next day they did meet again, and having some time at their disposal, they engaged in an

animated conversation about some pending legislation.

Colonel Hunt had insisted on bringing his
wife to Washington with him. They had rented
a quiet little furnished house, well-located and
at a reasonable rent, where they were living
very quietly, but very happily. Mamie was
rather enjoying her new situation and had formed
many pleasant acquaintances, among them being
the famous Countess Ilman, whom Mamie at
once decided to be one of the most pleasant ladies
she had met. Countess Ilman was one of those
ladies who have the power to charm at will. No
one could withstand the power of her blandish-
ments, when she chose to exert them. Mamie
fell an easy conquest, and Henry looked on with
a smile. Countess Ilman was received in the
best houses in Washington; she was pleasant,
accomplished, vivacious, amusing and very
pretty. Her father chaperoned her everywhere,
and she seemed to be the life of the circle she
moved in. And almost before she knew it, she
and Mamie were confidential friends. In fact,
it was the Countess Ilman who readily chose
most of her friends for Mamie, and was her
most valued instructor and adviser, in all of the
hundreds of little things on which Mamie needed
experience in entertaining and in all society

customs.   Mr. Lyman and the Countess Ilman
had both met at the residence of Colonel Hunt,
and then it was that the Countess had confided
to Mamie that she and Mr. Lyman were going
to be married during the holidays of Congress,
which were now only two weeks away.   This
news received due congratulations from both the
Colonel and his wife, and they readily accepted
an invitation to be present when the ceremony
was performed.

CHAPTER XI.

THE first month of Congress never amounts to much. The president's message is read, discussed and forgotten. Reports of the cabinet officers, ditto. The offices in both houses are filled, after a wrangle. The members are sworn in, seats are drawn for and swapped off. The new congressmen get acquainted and learn how to ride the congressional goat. A war or two is threatened and peace is restored. People wander around the galleries and wonder what on earth it all means. The hotels are all crowded and some greenhorn is continually getting into the wrong room, or blows out the gas, or rings the fire alarm in on all the guests, until finally the machine has ground out the committees and all the members kick up a row because they did not get on all of the committees. Then Congress adjourns for the holidays. A month has been used to do not over three days' work, but— it's the program and it is always carried out, to the letter.

Henry kept himself posted about all of his

brother's movements,and his continued success, both in Congress and in society, was as wormwood and gall in Henry's heart. Poor fellow! He was beginning to find out that there are some things in this world that money cannot buy,and that happiness was one of them. He knew that Mr. Lyman did not approve of his conduct towards his brother, and he felt that there was a coldness springing up between him and his partner, but he felt that he could not help it. He had forgotten that it was Mr.Lyman's hand and head that had landed him in his present position in life. Perhaps he did not know that it was Lyman's name that gave his bank its stability and reputation in the business world, but this was true. The reader must remember that the world knew nothing of Mr. Lyman's connection with the lobby at Washington. It must also be remembered that he made frequent visits to New York, where he was regarded as one of the shrewdest financiers in the metropolis.

Every man who perpetrates one outrageous wrong will have to prop it up with other wrongs,unless he has the moral courage to retrace his steps, acknowledge his error and correct it. Henry did not have this courage, so he had attempted to prop up his first outrage against his parents and his brother, by committing other

outrages against them. He had done this so long
now, that he felt that it was a personal injury to
him for any one else to be kind to them.   Mr.
Lyman's sympathies were with his partner's relations from the day that Henry refused to cancel the mortgages, as he had suggested, and the
breach was gradually widening between them.
On meeting Colonel Hunt and his wife, Mr.
Lyman was really charmed with them. So was
the Countess Ilman. A strong friendship sprang
up between these parties at once, and subsequent
acquaintance had ripened this into a lasting respect for each other.   Without knowing it,
Colonel Hunt and his wife were exerting a great
influence for good over Mr. Lyman and his future
wife.   The purity of the one was shaming the
baseness of the other.   This friendship had
awakened in the breast of Mr. Lyman and his
fiancée a desire to be really better and a feeling
that it was their duty to lead better lives.   Not
that either of them had ever been outrageously
wicked in any way, outside of the methods that
their business in life had caused them to adopt.
While the Countess Ilman had turned the
head of many a green legislator by her blandish-
ments, it had all been done for a purpose; it was
part of her business to do this. But in her private
life she had been as chaste as an angel.   In her

breast was a heart that beat as unselfishly and
as purely as that of a babe unborn. Mr. Lyman
had found out her sterling qualities and had
fallen in love with her. She had returned his
affection and they were soon to be married.
Colonel Hunt and his wife had won their entire
confidence and respect from the first, and no
thought of attempting to influence him, as lobbyists, had ever entered their heads. It was a
friendship of the purest sort, springing from the
best of motives. And it was a strange thing,
too, that the king and queen of the Washington
congressional lobby should feel such a great
friendship for the man and woman who were by
both inclination and position bound to be the
greatest enemies of that lobby. It was one of
the anomalies to be met with in politics everywhere. But as yet neither side of the contest
acknowledged the other as an opponent. Both
were on terms of neutrality at present, but each
of them was destined to feel the prowess of the
other, sooner or later.

Henry now did one more outrageous thing,
and made one more mistake. He wrote Mr.
Lyman a letter, saying that if it was his intention to invite his brother and his brother's wife
to the wedding, it would be impossible for him
to attend. This practically forced Mr. Lyman

to choose between his partner and his friend, and their families, as guests at his marriage; but the decision was prompt and effective. He wrote Henry a long letter, telling him that his brother had been invited and had accepted the invitation, so that it would be impossible to call the invitation off. He mentioned the fact that he had personally told Henry that he expected to invite Colonel Hunt and family, when he had invited Henry, and that no objection had then been raised. He regretted the unpleasant position that matters were in, and finished his letter with an invitation to Henry to drop the old feud and be reconciled to his brother. It was a manly letter to write, full of respect and careful of the feelings of the receiver, but it stung Henry to the quick and he resented it bitterly. He wrote a gruff note to Mr. Lyman, informing him that it would be impossible for him to attend the wedding, and extending congratulations in a formal fashion.

The wedding was a grand affair, but of a quiet order. They were married by a Chief Justice, in one of the leading churches, which was elaborately decorated. All of the leading members of Congress who had remained in the city, and a number of notables, were there. Colonel Hunt, although a married man, was pressed into the

services of best man, because the Countess insisted on having Mamie act as chief bridesmaid.
As a whole, the affair was a success, although
Henry and his wife refused to be present. However, as but little was known of them in Washington, this created very little talk.   During all
this time Colonel Hunt and his wife had no idea
that Mr. Lyman was Henry's partner, and as it
was March before the wedding tour ended, they
remained in ignorance of this important fact
until that time.

Mr. Lyman left another man in charge of the
lobby while he was gone on his wedding tour,
and as soon as Congress reassembled, this man
began work on the herculean task of "destroying the greenbacks."   He was not so astute as
Mr. Lyman had been, nor was he so able in his
management of affairs.   It so happened that the
lobbyists had secured exactly one-half of the
Committee on Finance and Banking to favor a
report asking Congress to call in the greenbacks.   The other half stood out against the
measure, and it required the vote of Colonel Hunt
to get the measure before the House.   Mr.
Green, the present manager of the lobby, was
in a sore perplexity. He had met Colonel Hunt
several times, and he felt a little afraid to ap-
proach him on the subject of a bribe, but it so

happened that he knew Henry Hunt, in New York, so he said to himself: "Henry Hunt would sell his chance of Heaven for money. This is his brother. I will risk it. I must have his vote. I will bid so high that none but a fool would refuse."

Accordingly, he called on Colonel Hunt and asked him to support the measure, saying, at the same time, that it would be worth $100,000 to him if he would vote for the measure and help him to pass it through the House. For a moment, Colonel Hunt felt like knocking the man down, then, on second thoughts, he answered: "If you desire my aid in this matter, you must first give me a full outline of your plans. I cannot afford to undertake to aid you unless I know all the grounds I am expected to travel over. Nor can I afford to go into it unless I know who will aid me to carry it through."

"Ah!" thought Mr. Green, "he is just like his brother. Wants to know all the ins and outs and chances of danger, but ready enough if it pays well and there is but little danger of detection!" With this idea in his mind, Mr. Green gave Colonel Hunt a detailed account of all of the lobby's plans, telling him that a majority of the members of the House owed their election to a promise made to the bankers in their home

districts, that they would vote for the recall of
the greenbacks, and a substitution of national
bank notes in their place.

"Give me a list of the names of these men,
that I may consult them before I decide," finally
said Colonel Hunt.

"Very well, sir; I suppose that I can trust you
to be very particular in this matter."

"Certainly."

With that a full list of the names and all par-
ticulars were handed to him; after which Mr.
Green asked him when he could see him again,
ready to pay the money, if Colonel Hunt was
satisfied to act.

"Two days hence, at this hour and at this
place."

"Very well, sir; I will be here, with the
money."

"God forgive me for this treachery, even to a
lobbyist, which I believe my duty demands!"
was the prayer of this noble-minded man, as he
retired that night, after thinking over the matter
in all of its phases, and deciding on his line of
conduct for the morrow.

Next day he called on every member named
in the list Mr. Green had furnished him, and
after giving the countersign and password,
found that they were all very willing to talk of

the matter, expressing themselves as ready to comply with their part of the program and vote for the measure, as soon as he should report it favorably to the House. They all seemed most anxious to get the matter attended to as quickly and as quietly as possible. And when Colonel Hunt asked them if they were not afraid that their constituents would hear of the measure and repudiate them at the next election, they all replied, as one man: "What do the common people know about such things? They cannot tell a bank note from a treasury note to save their lives. And what if they do hear of it. A bank note is just as good as a treasury note anyway!"

"But will it not give the banks the power to corner the currency, as well as the gold, at any time?"

"Oh, as to that, the banks will let us have all the money we can give them security for, anyway."

One big-hearted country greenhorn, whom the banks, out in some backwoods district, had elected to Congress, offered to loan the colonel his "book uv instrucshuns de banks give me afore they elected me," which was thankfully accepted by Colonel Hunt.

Colonel Hunt met Mr. Green at the appointed

place, and the following conversation took place ·

"Are you satisfied, Colonel Hunt?"

"I am, most assuredly.   Everything you told me is absolutely true."

"Then here is your money, sir. You will find one hundred one-thousand-dollar bills in that package."

"I do not doubt it, sir.   Many thanks."

"Oh, not at all.   When will you present the bill?"

"To-morrow afternoon at two o'clock. Have all of your men on hand.   I will present the bill myself, and expect to make a speech on it."

Around the memory of that famous day in February, all patriotic Americans ought to hang the emblem of Liberty, arising out of the Morass of Corruption, for then and there it was that one of the grandest fights for America, ever waged, was won by Col. Arthur Hunt.   Every member on the lobby list was in his seat, and all the galleries were crowded to suffocation by their friends. The silence of death fell on the house as Colonel Hunt arose in his seat and addressed the speaker.

"Mr. Speaker: I arise to a question of personal privilege. It is my painful duty to expose a plot against the rights of our people, which, in its awful effects on mankind, if carried out, makes me tremble even in contemplation of it.

Sir, I am in possession of incontrovertible evidence that will convict the bankers of the United States of electing a majority of the members of this present House of Representatives, for the express purpose, and on a regular contract, that they shall pass a law withdrawing all of our United States Notes, commonly call Greenbacks, from circulation, and substituting therefor, National Bank Notes. Yes, sir, and more than this! I hold in my hand a bribe of $100,000, which was given to me, as chairman of your Committee of Finance and Banking, to induce me to report favorably the bill which has been agreed upon by the conspirators, to accomplish this accursed result.

"And what is worse still, I stand prepared to prove that this present House of Representatives is honeycombed with corruption. It stands here as the servants of the bankers and the railroads, ready to do the bidding of their masters, as commanded to do by a lobby so bold and so grasping that it is now demanding that we shall turn over our last vestige of governmental money and allow the banks to issue a money that they can control for their own benefit and against the best interests of the people. I assert, sir, that it is impossible to get this present House of Representatives to pass one single law that is not dictated by the banks or the railroads.

"When our forefathers formed our Constitu-
tion, they expressly withheld the right to make
money from all parties and corporations, and
relegated to this Congress the power and the
duty to make and maintain the money of the
people. Preceding sessions of Congress have
farmed out this sacred right to a certain class of
our citizens, called bankers, who have grown
fat off the misfortunes of our people, which
their own accursed methods have fostered and
created. Not content with this, they have bribed
over one-half of the members of this present
House of Representatives, by electing them to
their seats on a promise that they will vote away
the only part of our currency that these bankers
cannot corner and control, for their own interests..

"We Americans have prided ourselves on our
'free and independent press' heretofore, but I
stand here to-day and denounce the great majority of our leading newspapers, as being under
the influence of those bankers so far that they
will not dare give this speech of mine, even as
a news item, to-morrow morning. I hold in my
hand a circular issued by the American Bankers'
Association of Wall Street, New York, which
gives instructions to all of the bankers of the
United States to patronize only such papers as

will advocate the withdrawal of all of the Greenback money from circulation, and to withhold
patronage from all papers that will not advocate
this measure. God knows that I do not blame
the poor papers, for they cannot live without the
patronage of the bankers, especially if the bankers should use their influence against them. We
must do away with the bankers, before we can
ever have a 'free and untrammeled press' again.
That much is certain.

"And this same circular goes still further, sir.
It instructs the bankers of the United States as
follows:

"'Let the Government issue the Coin and the
Banks issue the Paper Money of this country,
for then we can better protect each other. To repeal the law creating National Bank Notes, or
to restore to circulation the governmental issue
of money, *will be to provide the people with
money*, and will, therefore, *seriously affect your
individual profits, as bankers and lenders.* SEE
YOUR CONGRESSMAN *at once*, AND ENGAGE HIM
TO SUPPORT OUR INTERESTS, THAT WE MAY
CONTROL LEGISLATION!'

"My God, gentlemen! These are facts! Here
are the original documents. I stand here and
wave them in their faces. I here have a list
of the Congressmen of this present House of
Representatives, who, no longer than yesterday

and the day before, acknowledged to me that they had promised the banks in each of their districts that they would vote for the recall of the Greenbacks, and for the substitution of National Bank Notes in their place, before the bankers would agree to give their influence in favor of their election, and these men are prepared to carry out their part of this unholy contract, and expected me to report this atrocious measure favorably to them in this speech. If any gentlemen in this House doubt my statements, I will read the list of names in order to convince them. No one answers, so I will pass the list to any committee that may be appointed to investigate these charges, when called upon.

"No, gentlemen! I cannot report this measure favorably. I accepted your bribe-money only because it was necessary to do so, so as to complete my evidence against you, and shall hold it subject to the instructions of this House, as evidence. As for me and mine, I want nothing to do with it. I thank my God that I have never made a dollar that did not come to me honestly! It is my daily prayer that I shall never allow myself to be guilty of accepting one cent that I have not justly earned. I thank you, gentlemen, for your kind attention."

The Speaker, as is usual in such cases, appointed a committee, naming those who would have been criminated had these charges been properly investigated, to investigate the charges made by Colonel Hunt, and to report to the House their findings, at their convenience. And although Colonel Hunt watched the records of Congress carefully for many years, he never knew what that committee ever did do with those charges. However, he had the satisfaction of hearing one report that they made a few weeks later. They found "one J. W. Green, whereabouts unknown, guilty of offering a bribe of $100,000 to Col. Arthur Hunt, for reporting a measure favorably from the Committee of Finance and Banking, which bribe was delivered by him to the House of Representatives, with a forcible denouncement of said Green, and others, and which money is hereby recommended to be used, by this House, for the purpose of founding an Asylum for Indigent and Debilitated Ex-Congressmen, in Washington City." Which said asylum has never since been heard of by any one.

The morning papers next morning gave a short description of the way in which Col. Arthur Hunt denounced one J.W. Green for offering him a bribe to induce him to report a measure favorably, which he refused to do.

Now, for the benefit of those youthful states-
men who expect to some day set the walls of
Congress on fire by their eloquence in behalf of
the rights of the people, the author is compelled
to state that this was the last ever heard of one of
the grandest speeches ever made within the walls
of Congress, in behalf of the rights of the people. I have no doubt that this is the first mention
of it that the reader ever heard.   No, my dear
boys, it will not pay you to waste your breath on
such noble sentiments as these, before the members of any Congress assembled in the United
States in recent years.   It will be time and
trouble lost.   The place to make such speeches
as this was, is at home, before the people, who
are honest, and who believe that you will make
them in their favor in Washington.   But it is
never done any more.   Not since the days of dear
old Patrick Henry and Col. Arthur Hunt.

CHAPTER XII.

IF Bob Ingersoll will carefully consider the promise that God made to Abraham of old, and then trace its perfect and complete fulfillment up to the present time, it will surely stagger his agnosticism, even though it does not make him a complete convert to Abraham's God. It will be remembered that when Abraham had offered up his only son, Isaac, as a burnt offering, and had actually tied the boy to the bundle of fagots, and was stretching out his hand to slay the child, an angel of the Lord called to Abraham, "out of Heaven,"and said: "By myself have I sworn, sayeth the Lord, for because thou hast done this thing, and has not withheld thy son, thine only son: That in blessing I will bless thee, and in multiplying I will multiply thy seed as the stars of the heavens, and as the sand which is upon the seashore; and thy seed shall possess the gate of his enemies."

To-day the Jews are scattered over every nation on earth. They are, indeed, a "peculiar people," in that, although they have been min-

gling with all other races of people, they remain
Jews, retain their personality, as a people, and
all of their forms and customs, both religiously
and socially, almost without a sign of a change.
You may travel to the furthermost parts of the
earth; you may sail over all the seas; you may
enter the largest cities; you may stop in the
smaller towns of every nation and tribe, and
there you will find the Jews, busily engaged in
their promised "possession of the gates of their
enemies." And now a thinking man is bound
to believe that they have carried all of the better
portion of the goods of all other people out of
those "gates;" for to-day we see a Jew at the
head of the banks of England, France, Ger-
many, Russia, Italy, Spain, Turkey, and almost
all other nations; while here in the United States,
our President has been forced to apply to the
Jews to uphold our tottering treasury and stand
guard over it, in order to allow it to continue
in business at all. Not only do we find them at
the head of the banks of all nations, but, more
than this, we find them at the head of almost all
of our banks, of all kinds, and in all nations.

And, what is more serious, we find that it is
the cunning brain of the Jew which has created
and fostered the present banking systems of all
nations, so artfully arranged, and so consum-

mately carried out, that all the people of the world are paying heavy tribute to those same Jews, in interest and exchange, without knowing that they are doing so.

The stupidity of the people, on this point, is so great that even Bob Ingersoll must admit that nothing short of the will of an all-powerful God could manage to keep the great masses of our people from awakening from the sleep that has fallen over them, financially, and throwing off the yoke of this servitude.

Two words alone are needed to explain this extraordinary condition of affairs, and they are "Interest" and "Usury." By a concerted cunning, peculiar to themselves, the Jews have contrived to get all the people of the world to adopt a banking system that allows the Jews to receive the money of the world as deposits, and then loan it out to the world at a good interest, on their own account, which interest goes into the Jews' vaults, as clear profits. Every man who deposits money in a bank regularly, is sure to want to borrow some from the bank at times, and here is where the Jew catches his victim. While the Jew has had the use of the money of the depositor free of charge all along, as soon as the depositor happens to need a little money he is forced to pay the Jew a full round interest, and give him ample security, in order to get it. In this way, all men who handle much money are forced into this net of the wily Jews, and are compelled to pay tribute to the cunning and cupidity of "God's peculiar people." This banking system was not created in a day, nor in a year. It was created by the Jew a little at a time, and has been fostered by him during many years. The people have been played upon, and taught that the theories of finance are very intricate, and that it takes a lifetime to understand them, while, really, nothing could be simpler than this plan of the Jews to gain tribute from the people of the world. A Jew opens up a vault and offers to take care of his neighbors' money free of charge. His unthinking neighbors have no really safe place to keep it, so they gladly turn it over to the Jew, who, in turn, loans out a large part of it to some others of his neighbors, who happen to want to borrow. He always keeps a safe percentage of it on hand, so that he can deliver any amount called for by any depositor, at any time. He soon ascertains what his "average deposits" are, and then he learns how much his "average withdrawals" are, so he soon knows just how much of his neighbors' money he can keep loaned out all the time. If he can secure ten per cent interest per annum, in ten years he will have a total equaling the amount he has used, to say nothing of compound interest. His unthinking neighbor has received his money from time to time, as he needed it, and he sees no reason why he should complain, so the Jew grows wealthy and is credited with being a "great financier." But this continual drain on every country on earth, has now been going on so long that the Jew now finds himself the owner of more solid cash than all the rest of the world together. Not satisfied with all this, the Jews have organized, are buying up legislators, passing laws and creating conditions all favorable to themselves. They see that as they create a scarcity of money, men will give more of the products of human skill and labor for it. They are now the practical owners of most of the money in the world, so they are making "dear money" and "cheap labor," at an astonishing rate.

Gold and silver have been the only money, of final redemption, for many ages. The Jews saw that by demonetizing silver they would double the value of gold. So they have been hoarding gold for many years, and have, within the last half century or so, succeeded in the complete demonetization of silver in all of the leading nations of the world. The consequences have been that the Jew's gold has doubled in value, and he can now buy twice as much human comforts and human power with his gold, as he could have done before.

And the most astonishing fact of all is, that the people have always had it in their power to defeat the schemes of the Jews in this matter, by voting down his schemes, but they have never done so. In fact, they have never taken the trouble to inform themselves as to what the Jew was really up to. A few have, but it was such a sly trick that they have kept their mouths shut, and have gone into the banking business on their own account. It seemed to them that it was a much more desirable thing to take advantage of the Jew's shrewdness, and make some money themselves, than it was to expose the trick to their fellow men, and have the Jew kicked out. Of course that was not a very patriotic way to look at the matter—but then, no one has ever accused our bankers of being overly patriotic. They have patterned after the Jews, in more ways than one.

And it has come to pass that those bankers, who have sprung from our own people, are now joining hands with the Jews in their efforts to completely subjugate the rest of the world.

They have identified their interests with those of the Jews, and we now find them working, neck and neck, with "God's peculiar people," all trying to reduce the supply of real money more, and increase the amount of labor and skill that it takes to get it,—except through the banking channel. In fact, we see those of our own flesh and blood—for the Jew remains a Jew forever—now going to the Jew for their instructions as to the best way to accomplish their purposes. To all intents and purposes, we might just as well concede that all bankers are Jews in this respect, for they all work on Jewish methods now.

CHAPTER XIII.

At the next stockholders' meeting of the banks, Henry reported the following results: Deposits,$17,000,000; loans and discounts,$17,500,000 at 7 per cent; short-time brokerage, $500,000 clear profits, above all expenses of the bank; diamond brokerage, $500,000 clear, or a total profit of $2,225,000 clear, in one year.

Mr. Lyman reported: Deposits, $1,800,000; loans and discounts, $1,450,000 at 7 per cent; short-time brokerage, $50,000 above all expenses of the bank; profits from the lobby fund only $350,000, or a total of about $500,000, making a total profit for the partnership of $2,725,000 clear in one year. They then increased the capital stock of the New York bank to $7,500,000, voted themselves a salary of $600,000 each for the next year, for the old bank, and $50,000 each, for the new one. It was evident that Mr. Lyman was feeling blue. But he felt that it was incumbent on him to explain why his profits from the lobby fund had fallen so far short of his expectations, so he said: "Green proved to be a very expensive blunder. It was entirely his fault that your brother was enabled to expose our methods and ruin the business for a time. As soon as the banks heard of this exposure, we lost over half of our membership of the lobby, and the rest of the banks became very cautious. It is like pulling eye-teeth to get any funds out of them now, and I have been compelled to call off the fight against the greenbacks, for a time."

So Colonel Hunt's speech had had some effect, anyway.

At every session of Congress since that time this unholy fight of the bankers on the people's money has been renewed. John Sherman led it, while the Republicans were in power, and every hair on his hoary head could be counted with a service for the money-lords. He started out "poor but honest," and by untiring efforts he is now a millionaire—the owner of millions that were paid to him for fighting the greenbacks.

When Cleveland was elected, Sherman's mantle fell on his broad shoulders and no man has ever been more untiring in the service of his masters. The entire time of the present administration has thus been employed. Every message, every letter, every appointment, every bond-issue, every act of Congress which has

touched financial questions, has been in the interests of the bankers and money-lords and against
the best interests of the masses. No man can
point out a single act to the contrary. A very
few years ago the ex-sheriff of Buffalo was a poor
man. To-day he is the possessor of millions,and
it is now in order for some of his friends to explain where he got them. If Morgan is not his
New York partner, it is time the fact was pro-
claimed. It is said that the laborer is worthy of
his hire; so, if Grover Cleveland has not been
well paid for his services in behalf of the bankers
and money-lords, then he is the biggest fool
mentioned in all the annals of mankind.

But with all of this great opposition,the greenbacks are still in existence—the last vestige of
the people's money—the only money in existence to-day which the Shylocks cannot corner
and control in their own interests. And woe
be unto this fair land of ours if the people suf-
fer themselves to be robbed of it!

In the course of the passing years, Colonel
Hunt found himself the father of an interesting
family,which had had the happy effect of drawing him and his wife closer together in every
way. Two lovely boys, each named after their
grandfathers, with two sweet little girls, each
bearing the name of one of their grandmothers,

were the pride and delight of their parents' hearts.

Colonel Hunt had been re-elected to his seat in Congress so many times that it seemed to him that Washington was almost home—although he never saw the time that the old homestead in Missouri, for which he had such a struggle with his brother in his earlier life, was not the dearest spot on earth to him. He and his wife prided themselves on this farm, and lavished every care and attention that was necessary to keep it in first-class condition in every way. Fine blooded stock of all kinds were bred here under the management of an excellent tenant who had charge of it while its owners were away in Washington, and they spent the happiest days of their lives on the farm, each year, watching their children gamboling on the green, under the careful inspection of Pompey—whose chief delight lay in looking after them.

Pompey had become quite a character during those years, for he had been with the family at Washington, where he was not only a faithful servant, but where he had proven himself to be a valuable watch-dog, in regard to the actions of the other servants. He had listened and "took notes" all along, and now the man who bought Pompey for a fool, would have lost his money.

The old people were jogging along content-
edly, for after they succeeded in paying off the
notes given to Henry, they had been able to
make a living by renting their lands and raising
stock, without much worry. They were getting
a little feeble, but their kind old eyes always
had a welcome for Colonel Hunt and his family
which seemed to be very delightful to all parties.

Henry's name was seldom mentioned between
them. The old wound was healing, slowly,
under the effects of passing years, but it had
left an aching void in their hearts, which was
still sore; so the subject had been tabooed and
was seldom mentioned. Once in a while it
was impossible to keep Pompey from expressing
his feelings on this subject, but, usually, the
matter was never mentioned, even for months
at a time.

Henry Hunt had spent a life of wealth, but
his family had never been allowed the pleas-
ures of luxury. He had always dealt out the
necessities of life to them with a miser's hand,
although his pride had caused him to spend
enough to keep up appearances, at least. Cora
was now the mother of three children, two boys,
who were named after two English lords—which
class was greatly honored by Henry—and one
girl, Victoria, named, of course, for the queen
of England.

With all of his miserly ideas, Henry had several hobbies, all tending towards a monarchical form of government for the United States, under which he hoped to purchase a title and be accepted as one of the nobility. This being the case, it is easy to understand why he named his children after the English nobility.

However much it may have been gilded before company, life in the New York mansion had never been pleasant to contemplate, in private. Cora had become a querulous, quick-tempered, hasty, exacting woman, and Henry had positively refused to gratify many of her whims. She seemed to have but little love for her children, who were kept under the guard of a governess, a nurse or a private. tutor, in order to keep them out of her way. In spite of her wealth, she had never been able to enter the best society of New York, and it had always rankled in her heart that her sister Mamie had been accepted as one of the undisputed leaders in Washington society. It is true that Cora had been welcomed by many of the millionaire families of the city, but her own good sense had proved to her that she was only received by the wealthy Jews and speculators of Wall Street, simply because it was the interests of those people to receive the wife of a great banker that had caused them to open their doors to her. She had long since become disgusted with the shallowness and fickleness of that society. She had found that it was all vanity and the vanity of vanities. She knew that it was an article that was purchasable, and controlled alone by the size of the applicant's purse, and she often found herself longing for some little real human sympathy and love, all of which seemed to have been denied to her. Of course she could read novels and go to the theater and to entertainments of various kinds, many of which she did attend, but these things grew monotonous after a time. She had a proud spirit, a good conception of things in general, and was by no means a stupid woman. She had accepted the painful parting with her parents and sister, simply because she found that it was impossible for her to live in amicable relations with them, without very severe censure from Henry. Taken all in all, she had been a very suitable wife for Henry. She had not loved him enough to demand much attention from him and he had been too busy to expect much attention from her.

Henry Hunt had had two very severe trials on his faith and worship of the English nobility. First a certain "Lord Houghton" had honored him with several visits while in New York, at all of which Henry had spared no expense in lavish entertainment, and the two had become fast friends. After a time my lord succeeded in borrowing some $10,000 from Henry, on his mere note of hand, and after my lord had left for parts unknown, Henry found that no less than seven rich "suckers" had been taken in by the same game. Thus we see that an English "nobleman" need not go hungry in New York. There are plenty of people there who will honor him, if he will condescend to rob them. Such is life. Then, when my lord, the Duke of Marlborough, came over after the Vanderbilt millions and girl, Henry was very much astonished to find that my lord did not care to call on a mere banker at all. This was a great shock to him, but it gave Henry the idea of advocating a monarchical form of government for this country, under which he would be able to buy a title that would admit him to the homes of all the nobles of Europe. Hence his opposition to every act of this people under a republican rule.

Without going into minute details, we must attend the next five annual meetings of the stockholders of our two banks. The first one showed the following: Deposits, $22,500,000 in the New York bank, with loans of $22,500,-000 at seven per cent; short-time brokerage,

$750,000 above all expenses of the bank; diamond brokerage, $750,000 clear profits, making a total of $3,000,000 as clear profits for this bank, for this year.

The Washington bank reported: Deposits, $2,500,000; loans, $2,000,000 at 7 per cent; short time brokerage (which means money loaned on less than 30 days' time, at an exceedingly high rate of interest), $100,000; lobby profits,$260,000, or a total of $500,000 in profits. The capital of the New York bank was then raised to $10,000,000, while that at Washington was increased to $500,000. The salaries were raised to $1,000,000 for the New York bank and $100,000 each for the other.

The next report showed the following results:

New York: Deposits, $35,000,000; loans $33,-750,000 at 7 per cent; short-time brokerage, $1,000,000 clear; diamond brokerage, $1,000,-000 clear; total profits for the year, $4,360,000. Salaries voted, $1,250,000 each.

Washington: Deposits, $4,000,000; loans, $3,750,000 at 7 per cent; brokerage, $150,000 clear; lobby, $120,000, making a total of $500,-000 clear profits this year.

Total profits for the partnership, $4,860,000. The stock of the New York bank was made $15,000,000.

The next year gives this result:

New York: Profits on $45,000,000 equal $2,-750,000 at 6 per cent, and the two brokerages paid $1,250,000 each, making a total of $5,250,-000, as clear profits this year.

Washington: Deposits, $5,500,000; loans, $5,-110,000 at 6 per cent; brokerage, $200,000 clear; lobby, $250,000, making a total of $750,000 profits this year.

Total profits of the partnership this year, $6,-000,000.

The stock of the New York bank was made $20,000,000 and that of the Washington bank was raised to $1,000,000, and there was money left to throw at the birds.

Friend, go on and make the calculation. I cannot do it, for it makes my heart ache. But do not take my word for it; make the figures for yourself. Let Mr. Lyman resign from the Washington lobby and burn the pawnshops up, and then make some more figures. The result will surprise you. Take the published statements of your little banks around you, and figure on them. This will explain to you why the banker comes smilingly down at nine o'clock, and walks leisurely back at three o'clock, and still lives on the fat of the land; while you are forced to toil from daylight until dark for a mere living—and getting in debt at that, if you are not particular. Take the wheels out of your head, my dear old business man, machinist, carpenter, laboring man, or farmer. Cut the string your banker is pulling on your thinking machine, and make a few figures for your own benefit. Get a barber to cut the wool out of your eyes, so that you can see and think a little bit about your own condition. Wake up! The banker has a mortgage on you and your prosperity, and it behooves you to get to work. He has already made slaves and serfs out of millions of your fellowmen, and he is working the same game on you.

Reader, this picture is not overdrawn. There are hundreds of banks in these United States, whose rapid rise ought to put you to seriously thinking about this matter. Look at the men who, twenty years ago, were running small banks in our larger cities! To-day they are millionaires, many times over. The little one-story bank building has turned into a sky-scraper, and the little $100,000 capital stock of the bank has risen to the mighty $100,000,000. Some one owns this money—for every dollar of it is as good as cash, almost, for the banker is not taking many chances. Some one has lost all of this money. There is a trick, somewhere. We have been turned into a nation of borrowers, by the turn of some card that we have not understood.

America! That name has ever been a synonym of great prosperity, and all of its citizens ought to be able to shout out its glories to all comers now.

But stop! What is that roar that we hear? Oh, God! It is the mutterings of discontent. It is the angry roar of disappointment. It is the pleadings of the poor for work. It is the begging of the hungry for food. It is the sighing of the wretched for relief.

Millions of your fellowmen are anxiously inquiring why all of these things should come to pass, in the midst of the greatest crops, the most astonishing inventions and the most unheard-of production the world ever saw. Want sitting in Plenty's lap. Riot nestling on the bosom of Peace. Poverty pleading with Wealth. Reader, what on earth does it all mean? It is time that you were putting on your studying cap.

CHAPTER XIV.

TEN years have passed away. The capital
stock of the bank of Andrew J. Lyman & Co.,
of New York, is now $50,000,000, while that
of their branch bank at Washington is $10,000,-
000. Their average deposits are now about
$225,000,000, while their loans average about
$200,000,000 at 4 per cent interest per annum.
Their short-time brokerage pays them about
$6,000,000 per annum, clear, above all expenses
of the bank, while their diamond brokerage
pays about $6,000,000 clear profits. This gives
each of the partners an annual income of about
$10,000,000 each, and Henry actually smiles
as he thinks of that annual joke about being
president of these United States, at the insignifi-
cant salary of $50,000 per annum. It is the first
real smile that he has enjoyed for many months.
Usually his brows are contracted over some
question involving millions. This has become
such a habit with him that the skin on his forehead has turned into a complete set of deep
wrinkles, which he has the habit of changing,

first up and down and then crossways, according to the news that he has received. He is a terror to his help in the bank, and his wife and boy are as afraid of him as they would be of the evil one himself. He has gotten into the habit of scolding every one he comes in contact with, and the mere mention of the name of one of his relatives is enough to throw him into such a rage that it will take him half an hour to get out of it.

Mr. Lyman is in Europe, figuring on a big war loan to one of two belligerent nations, whose rulers have some little grievance or other against each other. He has just cabled Henry that he has agreed to carry some $50,000,000 in five-per-cents, fifty years, and Henry is unusually happy over it. The dogs of war will now be turned loose, and thousands will be slain, simply because a banker has seen a chance to make a profit out of the awful slaughter, and some little ruler has been snubbed by some other little ruler, both of whom would be afraid to attempt to settle the matter as men usually do. And when thousands have been slain, and the war has ceased, then millions of serfs will have to work for the interest on these same bonds, while their hearts are sore over the loss of many dear ones, who were *murdered* that this banker might

make his unholy gains. But why complain?
Such is life.

When Mr. Lyman returned, he was feeling
jubilant. He felt ready to commence his war
on the people of the United States again, now
that he had so successfully engineered a war in
Europe. "Well, Henry," he said, "what do
you say to going after those greenbacks again?
We have a new Democratic Congress, with a
President that is with us, teeth and toe-nails."

"It is now or never, sir, in my opinion."

"So I think. In order to accomplish our purpose, we must make hard times, take a lot of
these greenbacks, withdraw a lot of that 'gold
reserve' and force the government to issue
bonds, with which to redeem the greenbacks,
in order to get them out of the way and save the
gold that is now in the treasury. I have seen the
new President and his Secretary, and feel assured
they will never offer silver for these notes, for, if
they did, then our game would be blocked. This
would throw the country on a silver basis and
kill all of our schemes at once. But since I succeeded in demonetizing silver so easily, I have
no doubt that I shall be able to force the Government to call in the greenbacks, and let us issue
bank-notes in their place. I know that a panic
is a bad thing for banks, if it goes too far, but I

will be sure to be able to stop it before it reaches New York. I do not care if I do burst a few of the smaller banks, in the interior. There are too many of that class of banks anyway. Let the people learn to come here for their money, and make their deposits here. I have prepared a circular, which I wish to submit to you. Read it."

"Dear Sir:—The interests of National Bankers require immediate financial legislation by Congress. Silver, Silver Certificates and Treasury Notes must be retired and National Bank Notes, *upon a Gold basis*, made the ONLY MONEY. This will require the authorization of from $500,-000,000 to $1,000,000,000 of new bonds, *as a basis of circulation.* You will at once retire one-third of your circulation and call in one-half of your loans. Be careful to make a money-stringency felt among your patrons, especially among influential business men. Advocate an extra session of Congress for the repeal of the purchase clause of the Sherman law, and act with other banks of your city in securing a large petition to Congress for its unconditional repeal, per accompanying form. Use personal influence with your Congressman; particularly, let your wishes be known to your Senator. The future life of National Banks, as fixed and safe investments, depends upon your immediate action, *as there is an increasing sentiment in favor of Governmental legal-tender notes and Free Silver Coinage.*"

"I intend to have our American Bankers' Association sign this circular, and I will mail it to every National Bank on our lists at once."

The reader doubtless remembers the effect of this famous circular, for it caused the panic of 1893. The bankers were so eager to obey these instructions that they really overdid the matter of making "a money-stringency felt," for they caused millions to make a rush on the banks, which came very near breaking every bank in the country. Mr. Lyman was compelled to work every scheme known to his consummate ability, to keep his own banks from failing; but at last he struck the happy idea of issuing millions of dollars' worth of notes, signed by the clearing house of New York City, which is composed of all of its leading banks, and in this way, he succeeded in staying the curse of devastation that he had started going. Of course the people lost many billions of dollars of their hard earnings—but the purchase clause of the Sherman law was repealed. However, there was still enough manhood in that Congress to refuse to destroy the greenbacks, which are now the last vestige of our money that the banker cannot control. Onslaught after onslaught was repulsed, and at last the lobbyists were forced to retire defeated.

It cost this nation the greatest panic the world ever saw to repeal the purchase clause of the Sherman law, which every thinking man in the country, outside of those influenced by the banks, wanted to change into a law for the absolute free coinage of silver, which had been stabbed in 1853, and murdered, without the knowledge of its friends, in 1873.

When the author of this little book published this circular, soon after the panic had ceased, it was denied by the bankers of New York, but he stands ready to prove that this circular was issued, as stated, in exactly the words given above. No mere flippant denial of it will be received, when the above words were copied from one of the original circulars, with this writer's own hand, and he stands ready to testify to all of the facts, giving all of the details except the name of the banker who kindly let him see it, which the author is under a solemn promise to keep sacred.

But to any thinking man, does this circular need further proof than merely to point out the immediate results of it—the panic?

It is true that this country was running on declining prices, caused by the demonetization of silver in 1873, but it was in a tolerably prosperous condition in 1892. Its wonderful resour-

ces had been able to keep it out of serious financial storms before that time, although the bankers had drawn billions of dollars from the life-
blood of its commerce. But there was no
outward visible reason why this panic should
have come, just when it did. No sensible man
can be convinced that it was not caused by the
above circular, once he thinks of the matter in
all of its bearings.

The calling in of the funds, as indicated in
this circular, caused the panic, even before the
purchase clause repeal could have effected it.
It is true this repeal caused the people to awake
to the fact that silver had been demonetized, and
this aggravated the causes of the panic, but the
panic itself was started by this circular, as Mr.
Lyman desired that it should be started, when
he sent it out.

CHAPTER XV.

AFTER the famous battle that Colonel Hunt led in the House of Representatives, in behalf of the greenbacks, in 1893, he was honored as few men in his position ever were honored before. Almost the entire country, outside of the banker and his influence, rose up, regardless of political lines, to do him honor. His name was mentioned freely as a possible candidate for the presidency, and there could have been no man selected who would have been as universally popular with the masses; but he was too well posted to entertain the matter for a moment. He knew that it was impossible for any man to be elected president of the United States, who opposed the banks. He knew their power and influence better than the people did, and he would not allow himself to lead a forlorn hope. The truth of the matter was that he was sadly disappointed, not at his own career, but at the results of it. He had unselfishly and honestly applied himself to his work. He had done all that he could to stay the hand of the destroyer. He had fought the powers of oppression with all of his might for twenty-six years, while in Congress. He had never seen the time when he would not have given his life, freely, if by so doing he could have saved the people from the awful destruction the bankers were preparing to deal out to them.

But he had been defeated. He saw that he was too weak to withstand their onslaughts much longer. He saw the time was near at hand when the people would be compelled to arouse themselves, or else be slaves.

Colonel Hunt offered a bill for the re-establishment of the banking business of the United States, on the following lines, during the last session of Congress: After repealing all con flicting laws, it gave the land-owners of every county, town, district, city ward, or other subdivision of any city, containing 5,000 inhabitants, the right to vote for a Governmental Bank of Deposit, which shall be established by the Government of the United States, when one hundred or more of the land-owners in the com munity named shall subscribe their names to the stock of said bank, which shall vary, according to the desire of the subscribers, from $10,000 up to $500,000, which stock shall not amount to more than one-tenth of the actual cash value of the property of the subscribing stockholders, all of which must be free and clear from all en-

cumbrances of any nature at the time of the subscription, the Government to have a first lien on
all of the property named to the amount of the
subscription made by its owner, to secure it from
all loss on account of the bank.   When all of
this has been approved by bonded examiners of
the Government, then the Secretary of the
Treasury of the United States shall issue to said
bank the amount of its stock, in either Gold or
Silver or Treasury notes receivable for all debts,
dues and demands in the United Sates, but
which shall not draw interest, and shall issue a
charter for same and turn it over to the managers
of said bank, which will then be ready to begin
business.   The stock of said bank shall be duly
recorded in the mortgage records of the county,
and then held by the United States as a lien on
each piece of property mentioned for the amount
named against it, and shall not be released until
this amount, together with all expenses of this
transaction, shall have been paid, in exactly the
same kind of money that the bank has received
from the Government, when a full release may
be issued.

This bank, when so chartered, shall have the
right to receive deposits, loan money on approved bankable paper and do a general banking business; but after paying all expenses of

running the business, including reasonable salaries to competent managers, clerks, etc., together with four per cent per annum interest to all of the land-owners interested, according to the amount of stock which they own, then the remainder of all profits shall be divided between all of the depositors, according to the amounts of their average deposits during the year, on the basis of monthly exhibits, as follows: A depositor who has an average of $100 in the bank all of the time, of every month in one year, shall be entitled to the same share as a depositor who has had $1,200 in the bank all the time for one month, etc.

The Government assumes no responsibility for any action of any officer of the bank, nor does it guarantee any depositor against loss, but every depositor shall have a second lien on the land which is covered by the first lien of the Government's, to secure him against loss if the bank fails, said second lien to be subject only to the lien of the Government; said land to be appraised by Governmental bonded inspectors, who shall require sworn valuations from its owner and three of his adjoining neighbors, when appraised.

Then followed clauses to prevent fraud and punish offenders, to elect officers by a majority of

all of the stock-owners, to assess all of the banks
an annual tax sufficiently large to pay the Government for all expenses incurred in looking
after the banks, etc., but which was in no case
to exceed one per cent per annum of the amount
advanced by the Government to the bank.

Then followed a clause opening the mints of
the United States to the free and unlimited
coinage of both gold and silver, at such a ratio as
may from time to time be required, to keep the
international, intrinsic value exactly with the
coinage value.   Subsidiary silver coins to be on
equal proportionate weight and fineness with
other silver coins.   The government to immediately coin all of the silver in the treasury, and
begin recoining all silver coins, as fast as they
are received, into coins of the proper weight
and fineness to keep the intrinsic value of the
two metals the same as the coinage value, as
nearly as possible.   All holders of our present
silver coins to have the right to send them to
the mints and get the same number of new coins
—the Government to stand all loss, if any.

Then followed a clause ordering the Government to issue an amount of treasury notes equaling the whole amount of the public debt, requiring the banks to buy enough of those notes, all
along, to pay off the public debt as fast as it

falls due; if gold be needed, then in gold; if silver be needed, then in silver, or, if treasury notes be needed, requiring the holders of the bonds to accept treasury notes from the Government.

Then followed a clause giving to the debtor the right to pay all debts, dues and demands he owes or may owe, in either one of the kinds of money mentioned above, unless the original note or bond calls for one special kind of money. This privilege was also given to the Government, as well as to all other debtors.

Then 'followed a clause forbidding the Government to issue more than an amount of treasury notes equaling all of the gold and silver together, now in circulation, or thereafter to be placed in circulation.

Next came a clause making it the duty of all officers inspecting goods for export, to collect five per cent export duties on all money shipped out of the United States to any foreign nation.

Next came a clause making it high treason against the Government to be guilty of trying to increase or decrease the value of the Government's money, by any device, trick, scheme, trust, combination or condition whatsoever, punishable all the way from a small fine, in small cases, to expulsion from the country in larger cases. Very severe punishment was to be meted out to all bankers who defalcated, or caused any depositor or the Government any loss through any trick, scheme, trust, combination or condition, whatsoever.

The old banks were given a reasonable time to wind up their business and retire—although this was unnecessary, for they would find themselves without depositors as soon as the new banks could get started going.

Every possible precaution was taken to prevent fraud. All possible safeguards were thrown around it. This bill was the careful thought of one who had spent a lifetime in studying the matter, and it will certainly pay the reader to study it over carefully. Some bill, like this, must be passed soon to save our country from the clutches of our present grasping bankers' greed.

Colonel Hunt's speech in advocacy of this bill was the master-work of his life, and it was sent to the uttermost parts of the country and used as one of the strongest arguments of the times. Of course it created a great sensation, and no wonder, for here are a few excerpts from it:

"Mr. Speaker:—The political events of the last few years have opened the eyes of this people to the fact that they have been mercilessly robbed, . through the acts of this

Congress. Yes, sir, I repeat it! Robbed in cold blood, by those they have trusted and whose duty it was to protect them. Look, sir, at the Senator from Ohio (Sherman) and those of his financial clique—every one of them millionaires. They demonetized silver and have received their reward.· They have sold their constituents for a price, and now have the blood money in their possession. Their price was high, but the money-lords could well afford to pay it. And then, sir, look at the fact that those same money-lords have made the common people believe that Sherman was a statesman—by using the columns of a partisan press, which was forced to laud him up to the skies, to keep the people from learning the real facts and crushing both him and his press supporters, for their treachery. But now a day of reckoning is at hand.

"Then cast your eyes on the ex-sheriff from Buffalo! Unknown, unnoted and unsung, he sprang from obscurity into prominence, simply because he espoused the cause of Wall Street, against the people, and has had the backbone to deliver the goods. Yes, sir, I repeat it! Cleveland has delivered us over to our enemies —and is to-day a millionaire, beloved of all the gold-bugs, and a saint and an angel in the eyes

of the Shylocks.   Private bond-contracts in a
public office!   Ye gods!   A self-acknowledged
traitor, who accepted the nomination on a bi-
metallic platform and then ran our government
on a gold basis—obtaining a large amount of
the yellow metal as his part of the vicarious sac-
rifice.   Cleveland, the man who has insisted on
paying out gold for silver certificates and issuing
more bonds for more gold to pay out for other
silver certificates, all positively against all law
and all equity, simply because the bankers have
demanded a billion dollars' worth of bonds, to
be used as a banking basis. Ah! what a servant
is this!   Ever ready to obey the behests of his
masters, even though he has to perjure his soul
by turning traitor to his oath of high office—
supposed to be the most sacred oath known to
our language. And had we a Congress of Wash-
ingtons, Jeffersons, Henrys, Jacksons, Calhouns,
Clays and Lincolns, he would be impeached
and in prison before the sun sets this day.

"It is with a feeling of horror that I refer to
the present Secretary of the Treasury.   A sad-
ness comes creeping over me, as I consider his
poor predicament—his conscience a seething
mass of the flames of torment, his poor trembling
soul shuddering on the brink of the inevitable
chasm of public condemnation, after a long life

in the honorable service of his state, he is doomed to die in the slough of despond, penniless, friendless and accursed—and all because he obeyed his master too well!

"History is now about to repeat itself. Remember the fate of Babylonia, of Assyria, of Persia, of Greece, of Rome and of Carthage. As long as they were well governed by honest officials they prospered, but after the Shylocks had bought up their legislators and had grown wealthy off the spoils of the people, they all withered and died in their own wickedness, while the hordes of hardy men from the hills and the frontiers formed themselves into armies and overthrew them. Their ill-gotten gains were scattered to the four winds of the earth, and history gives us their names as a warning. And well will it be, sir, if we take warning from the present breeze, which but now indicates the rising of the awful storm of death and destruction. If we do not, then look out for the hardy men of the hills, who are even now practicing with their weapons in contemplation of coming events. Poor, foolish Coxey had the idea in a modified form, but the Tamerlane of the hills will be a very much more determined person, one who will not only step on the grass, but who will also boot the members of this Government out of their offices and loot the strong-boxes of the Shylocks, as his predecessors did the Greeks and the Romans of old. Ah! you smile, but let me tell you millionaires that, unless you loose your hold on the throats of the people, my words will return to you, when it is too late, with all the force of a prophecy in them. Think not, ye Shylocks, that the day will not come when the aggressiveness of an outraged people will dethrone you from the high seats you have stolen and obtained by bribery and corruption. And may God have mercy on you, when it comes.

"The political parties all lead to the Shylock's office. They all get the money from the money-lords to carry on the campaign with—and the misers always obtain a good interest on their money. The politicians are compelled to serve their masters, because their living depends upon it. Personally, these politicians had rather serve the people, if the pay was as good, so we must make it our business to see that those who stand up for our rights are paid for it, and that those who have sold out their constituents are punished. All men serve a good paymaster, and as long as the Shylocks pay the politicians, just so long will they dictate our laws and rob us by rote. Just so long will we find it impossible to change our present iniquitous banking laws and stop the immense interest now going to the banker, made by the money of the depositors, none of which goes into the pocket of its owner.

"To illustrate, let us take, for example, the National Bank of Commerce, of Kansas City, which has a capital of $1,000,000, with a surplus of $200,000 and deposits amounting to $4,-500,000, giving its officers absolute control of $5,700,000 in cash, all the time. Of this they loan about $4,250,000 at an average rate of— well, say eight per cent, but those who borrow it will swear that it averages twice that rate—or more. This gives this bank $340,000 income per annum. Let us then assume that the *legitimate* expenses, not including salaries of officers, are $40,000 per annum. This leaves us $300,000, as interest on capital and official wages. $1,200,000 at eight per cent makes $96,000, which gives an ample interest on all the capital invested in this bank, which, taken from the $300,000, leaves us the enormous amount of $204,000 clean, clear cash which these half-dozen men are receiving every year, as official wages from this bank. I cannot help wondering how they divide it up. Let us see; there is Dr. W.S.Woods,who is president. He owns a controlling interest in the bank, that is evident, and as we know he is a greedy cuss, we will give

him, say half of it, or an annual salary of $100,-
000, or just twice as much as this United States
is paying the President. W.A.Rule is cashier.
He is a mighty handy little man, and although
he does not own a great deal of stock, still we
feel that he ought to be paid as much as the
United States is paying its Secretary of the
Treasury, which is $8,000 per annum. To the
first and second vice-presidents we will pay
the same, $8,000 per annum each. This will
enable us to pay to the other twelve directors
exactly the same wages that the United States
is paying to its Congressmen, and after paying
all of these munificent salaries, we will have
plenty of money left to pay a large assessment
- from the lobby at Washington 'and for other
purposes.'

"My God, gentlemen! does this seem like
hard-times wages? Would you have me believe
that times are hard when such ordinary, average
men as these gentlemen are, can make such
wages as these are? No, sirs, the times are
flourishing in the National Bank of Commerce
at Kansas City. They are in clover. They are
dressing in fine linen and living off the fat of
the land, these gentlemen bankers are. They
toil not, neither do they spin, but the world is
theirs and they have a down-hill pull on it, at

that. But this is not all. There are thousands
of other similar institutions in this country and
they are all faring sumptuously. This illustra-
tion fits them all, except in details. They do not
know that we are having hard times in this
country. If you will go with them to their man-
sions you will find that their wives and daughters
are the proud peeresses of our land. They spend
their days trying to invent some new, ingenious
and untried way to spend their surplus wealth.
They eat their meals off solid silver and dec-
orate themselves with solid gold. Well trained
servants glide over their marble halls, ready to
do the bidding of the masters who pay them a
pittance for it. And I ask you, gentlemen, to
remember that this is the case in those pampered
homes in this year of our Lord, 1896, when the
farmer's corn is only worth 15 cents per bushel.
This is the way our bankers and money-lords
are living, while the poor old farmer is trying
to sell a good horse for $10 to pay his taxes with,
and can scarcely find a purchaser at that price.
Gentlemen, this is the condition of our Shylocks, while millions of our populace are tramp-
ing the sidewalks of our cities begging for work
at any price, and tens of thousands of honest men
are trudging over our muddy highways, begging for bread. Thus are the money-changers

faring, while millions of our defenseless women
and children are huddled together in the hovels
of the poor, not knowing where the next meal
is to come from.

"But, you say, where is the remedy for all of
these evils? I will tell you in a nutshell. Listen:
1st. Give us absolute Governmental money, free
coinage of both gold and silver at the proper
ratio, whatever that may be, and Government
legal-tender greenbacks, in sufficient volume to
do all of the business of the nation and of the
people on a cash basis. Burn every bank-note
in existence and make it high treason for any
person or corporation to attempt to issue anything in the shape of money, in any way. Place
heavy penalties on all persons found guilty of
attempting to increase or decrease the money of
this nation in any way, and fix a heavy export
duty on gold and silver to be shipped out of this
country. 2nd. Establish banks on the basis of
the bill I have presented here, thus giving each
depositor the interest on his own money, when
loaned out by the bank, and also placing the
banking basis on the solid values of well located
real estate at such a vast per cent discount of its
real value that it will be impossible for tricksters
to cause loss to the Government or to depositors.

"The cause of all the trouble has been in

three evils which can be easily remedied: 1st.
The great appreciation of primary money, gold.
Remedy, both gold and silver, as absolute money
for all purposes. 2nd. Our present system of
banking was made by the money-lords and is
being run in their interests altogether, and
against the interests of the masses. Remedy,
the bill I have presented and which I have
heretofore explained fully. 3rd. This Government has farmed out its own inalienable rights
to make and maintain the money of its people,
a medium of exchange that shall be unchange-
able in value at all times, to a set of men who
have manipulated the money of this country in
such a way that we now have 4,000 millionaires
who own more than one-half of all the total
values of all kinds in this country, while some
65,000,000 of our people are now on the verge
of bankruptcy, ruin and starvation. Remedy:
Take back this, the most sacred power of our
Government and let the United States make and
maintain all of its own money, both coin and
paper, and throw such safeguards around it as
will forever destroy the power of our oppressors.
Sweep the national banks out of existence, and
thus, at one fell swoop, destroy the most power-
ful monopoly that ever existed on the face of
the earth. Do these things, gentlemen, and you

have solved the problem of our prosperity as a nation and a people. Refuse, and you will have to answer for it ere long, when the hosts of the Commune, the hordes of Attila and the bands of the Tamerlane of the hills have swooped down upon you and have drenched your fair land in blood and destruction. Oh, ye pampered aristocrats of the East, ye lenders of money and ye speculators in the rights of the masses, listen now to the notes of this warning; for when an outraged people once finally decide that they cannot get their rights by peaceable means, then will the worm turn on you with the cry of Vengeance! And the beast of burden will fall upon you and destroy you, and your palaces shall be made waste places and your millions shall vanish into thin air!"

CHAPTER XVI.

THE total values of every kind of property in the United States, that is, the total value of all property of every kind and nature, is estimated at $40,000,000,000 (forty billion dollars), and now we have about 4,000 men who own about $25,000,000,000 (twenty-five billion dollars') worth of it. Query: How long will it take these four thousand men to get all the rest of the property in the United States?

Let us figure on this proposition a little. Say they get four per cent interest on their money per year, then we find that twenty-five billion dollars will bring them just one billion dollars interest at four per cent; so, as the other 65,-000,000 people of this country now only own fifteen billion dollars' worth of property in this country, it will only take these four thousand men fifteen years to get all of it, to say nothing of compound interest.

In fifteen years, then, four thousand men will own every dollar's worth of property in this United States.

You do not believe that, do you?

No, kind reader, that is not true; but here is the reason of its apparent falsity. If all of the workers of the United States could stop work for fifteen years, then these four thousand men would, undoubtedly, own every dollar's worth of property in the United States within the term of fifteen years, provided they could collect the interest on their investments.

But these four thousand men have about 65,000,000 slaves at work for them. These slaves ought to produce, we will say, a profit of say $10 per head each year. This means $650,000,-000 per annum to be taken out of the billion dollars our masters are demanding from us each year, which leaves only $350,000,000 per annum which will have to be taken out of our property to pay to the Shylocks, after they have taken all of the profits of all of our labor.

If they get $350,000,000 worth of our property every year, how long will it take them to get all of the rest of our fifteen billion dollars' worth still left to us?

About forty-three years.

Is that all?

Yes, that is all. They will own every dollar's worth of property in the United States in forty-three years, provided values rise fast enough to pay the compound interest; if not, then in much less time; unless we have a change in our present financial policies.

Yes, I know you cannot believe this, but then, you know, "figures cannot lie."

Prepare your necks for the yoke, for the burden is falling on you; nay, it is already firmly fastened on you and your children.

And still ye are Democrats! Yaller-dog Democrats!

Or perhaps ye are Republicans! "Wahhosses," eh?

"Daddy carried his pumpkins to the house with a pumpkin in one end of the sack and a rock in the other, and I guess he knew what he was doing."

Certainly. Your father was a very wise man, when compared with the son he has raised. No doubt about that.

———

What is interest?

It is the penalty we have to pay for being poor.

But the really poor cannot borrow, without security.

No, but they are better off than the man who is just rich enough to be able to borrow, and poor enough to be forced to do so; for interest is but the knife of the cold-blooded Shylock, with which he cuts out his pound of flesh. There is no poison so deadly to prosperity as the poison of interest.   It withers up and dies as soon as the Shylock's knife is laid at its roots.   Debt is the death-dealing quagmire that has sunk millions in the slough of despond, after the Shylock's knife, interest, has cut away all of the arteries of life.   Friends, flee from debt, as you would from the demon of destruction. It is the only way you can beat the Shylocks.

We are a nation of borrowers.

Our law-makers have made us such.

Every law that has been passed within the last twenty years, touching finance, has been dictated by the bankers and money-lords.

They demonetized silver.

They planned the present system of banking.

They are demanding bonds—and they are getting them.

They have a patent-right on legislation of this kind.

They own the Democratic party.

They own the Republican party.

They own the executive.

They own Congress.

Friends, think you they will deliver up all of

these goods and chattels without a fight? No, never.

Then let us fight them.

Ah, there's the rub. Will we do it?

We must, or else be slaves.

———

What is $1,000?

The price of two able-bodied men.

How so?

It will make as much clear profit as they can. It is even better than the men, for it will not wear out and it never gets sick. It works every hour, wet or shine.

What has caused this to be so?

The great appreciation of our money, which has been manipulated by the money sharks, while honest men were at work. We have been robbed while asleep.

How was this done?

By demonetizing silver and cornering gold. By having the Government call in all of its own money and getting the right to substitute bank-notes for it.

———

What is money?

Gold and silver coins and legal-tender green-backs. It is simply a medium of exchange, manufactured by the Government, to expedite exchanges of values among its people.

What are bank-notes?

They are substitutes for money. They are notes given by banks, which agree to pay you the money for them on demand. The banks give the government security that they will pay them promptly, when presented, and then loan them out to the people, at big interest.

Are bank-notes as good as legal-tender greenbacks?

Certainly not. When a bank issues its notes it is going in debt for every dollar it issues. Say it has $50,000 capital and issues $45,000 worth of these notes, as is the case under our present law, you see it only leaves a margin of $5,000 above its debts, in case it should get into trouble. Would you not rather have the real money, issued directly from the Government, which is made a legal-tender for all debts, dues and demands in the United States, both public and private, than to accept the notes of a concern that owes within ten per cent of all that it is worth? Of course you would.

But the government's bonds are behind these bank-notes. Does that not make them good?

Certainly. But why is it necessary to have the bank-note at all. If the Government must secure the issue of the bank-notes, by selling the banker its bonds, and then pay him four per cent interest on the bonds, beside allowing him to loan the bank-notes out to the people at interest, why not have the Government issue the non-interest-bearing legal-tender notes itself, thus saving all interest and extra trouble?

Oh, you love the banker, do you? You want to force the Government to pay him interest and give him a nice soft snap all free of charge to him, do you?

Did you ever borrow money from a banker and find out just how much he loves you? Did you? Did he offer to pay you interest if you would agree to carry his notes for him? Ah, no. He demanded interest from you for the loan of his own promises to pay you the money on demand, now, didn't he? Yes, sir; he wanted you to pay him interest on his own debts, on his own notes, before he would let you have them. And then, about the security; did you ever have a banker stand up and tell you that your own credit was not worth a cent and that you must give him gilt-edged security before he would loan you some of his own debt-bank-notes? The very proposition is an insult to our American manhood and Government, which declares that all men are equal, and yet, here we have one

man stand up and proclaim his own greatness
and financial glory,while he is humbling that of
his neighbor in the dust, by his demands for security. And yet our Government is actually paying this man four per cent interest to do this.
It has given him a monopoly of our money and
forces us to bow down our heads and beg for
favors.

And all this makes you love the banker, does
it?

Ah, surely you are with me on this proposition, my friends. You have never thought of it
before, but now, since I have called your attention to it, I know that you will join me in this
matter.

We must wipe these national banks from off
the face of the earth. They are a menace to
our very existence. They have all joined hands
and now form the greatest monopoly on earth.
By concerted action, they have demonetized
silver, thus destroying one-half of our money at
one fell swoop, and doubling the value of every
dollar and debt that was due to them. They
have cornered the gold and are now clamoring
for the withdrawal of the greenbacks, because
they cannot control and corner them, and now,
every few months, we see them bleeding our
Government for hundreds of millions of dollars'

worth of bonds, under the efficient management of Mr. Cleveland and his cohorts. No stage robber ever held up a stage and demanded the money of the passengers more deliberately than the Shylocks are holding up our government and robbing it during these troublous times.

And still you love the banker, do you? Surely not.

—

What is a banker?

These are a set of men to whom the government of the United States pays four per cent interest and gives them a monopoly of handling its money, and the money of the people, because the people love them so well.

ᴴ But do they not pay the Government something for all of these great and special favors?

No, nothing except a very small tax, about the same as other people pay.

What is their business?

They are schemers and monopolists. They spend their time scheming out some new method of robbing the people who love them so well. They have combined and now have a complete monopoly of all of the money of this country, which they are now using to bleed this Government, by forcing it to issue hundreds of millions of dollars' worth of interest-bearing bonds, which they expect to use in forcing this nation to perpetuate their own existence, as the only purveyors of our money.

Why do the people love these bankers so well?

Because they are bankers and are rich and smart. The people of this country think so much of them that they are now depositing all of their money in their banks, all the time, free of charge, and are then borrowing this money back from the bankers and paying them the munificent sum of $360,000,000 per annum as interest on it. Not only that, but the people are insisting that the Government shall pay these bankers four per cent interest, per annum, on all of their capital, as interest on the bonds which the Government issues to secure their bank-notes with. Yes, and more than this, this Government is now giving these bankers an absolute monopoly on handling all the money used in this country, absolutely free, when this privilege would bring hundreds of millions of dollars, if offered to the highest bidder, as other Governmental contracts are let.

The bankers are the special favorites of the Government and the people of this United States. They have a very nice, soft snap and they are using it for all it is worth, while it lasts.

Is there no way to stop them from committing all of these outrages on the people?

Certainly. The people could vote them out of existence in two years' time, if they wanted to do so.

Why do they not do so?

Because they love the bankers so well. This is the only reason why they do not do so, that I can see.

Friends, I do not love the bankers so well, do you? If not, then we must get together and vote them out of existence. Will you help me? Ah, that's the question.

You must decide it for yourselves. God help you.

———

My story is told. Henry and Cora are still in New York, living in splendid misery. With all of their millions I extend to them my sympathies. They were not naturally bad. The business of their lives may have warped their dispositions. I believe it did. At all events, I am sorry for them. Their children are beautiful to look at, but under the circumstances surrounding them, we cannot expect them to be other than vain, frivolous and empty-hearted. Let us hope that they will not turn out to be vicious, from the same causes.

Colonel Hunt and his family are now in Washington, where he is still championing the great bill that he introduced, which has been fully explained heretofore. I do not know a happier family. The sweet bonds of sympathy and pure love bind them together with bonds that nothing but death can sever. The children, living in this heaven on earth, being reared by such a mother and father, are like the brightest and most beautiful blossoms on the Tree of Promise; and in after life will take their places in the world as worthy representatives of their parents.

The old grandparents are all still alive, happy and contented. They have thousands of bushels of this Democratic corn at 15 cents a bushel, plenty of three-cent pork and two-cent beef, and other edibles in abundance, and while they are not selling anything at present prices, they are living in the hope that Colonel Hunt may get his great bill passed and made into a law; when they confidently expect much better prices.

Mr. Lyman is still at the head of the lobby at Washington, which he reports as being in a very thriving condition, on account of the unusual activity that it has influenced Mr. Cleveland to make in the interests of the banks, in issuing the bonds so promptly when called upon. He is still fighting those legal-tender greenbacks, and says that he considers his efforts to have them withdrawn from circulation, as the only failure he has made in a long and eventful life. Still he does not despair of success yet. He and Mr. Cleveland stand very close together and are firm friends. In fact, I might say, I believe that he is acting as the President's Privy Counselor on Finance at this time. At all events, Mr. Lyman declares that Cleveland is the greatest statesman who has ever filled the White House, and all of the bankers, Shylocks and money-lords are echoing the sentiment in enthusiastic tones. There is one point that is a certainty—Wall Street stands up firmly and forever for the firm of Lyman and Cleveland. And so do England and the Shylocks of Europe.

"You Shelbina! You better keep outen dem jelly and cakes, er I'll tell Miss Mamie on yer. Dey weren't made fer sich niggers as you is ter ete. Deys made fur de white fokes, and—"

"Now, Pompey, you wouldn't tell on *me*, now wud yer?"

"Git erway from here gal, git erway, I tell yer! I ain't none uv yer hired servants, what yer kin buy off wid er smile an' er nudge. I'se one uv de family, I is, an' I don't 'pose to have yer wastin' de vittels dat way.   I'se one uv de family, I tell yer.   Git erway!"

And Pompey was the happiest darky in Washington.

THE END.